Donna Parker

at Cherrydale

By
MARCIA MARTIN

Illustrated by
JON NIELSEN

WHITMAN PUBLISHING COMPANY
Racine, Wisconsin

CONTENTS

1. Farewell to Friends 9

2. A Surprise Camper 21

3. Plans Change 35

4. Cherrydale 45

5. The Children Arrive 57

6. A Disappointment 76

7. Hot Weather Problems 95

8. The House in the Woods 110

9. The Boys from Three Pines 129

10. The Day Off 147

11. Johnny Disappears 158

12. Nancy Bond's Strange Illness 168

13. The Square Dance 185

14. Someone on the Stairs 202

15. Bunny's Problem Solved 209

16. The House Again 222

17. The Man on the Bridge 233

18. A Rosebud Opens 242

19. The Big Day 253

20. The Mystery Is Solved 269

CHAPTER 1 *Farewell to Friends*

"Twenty to the left, thirteen to the right, around once and stop at five."

Donna Parker bent her dark head over the combination lock on her school locker, and recited the numbers.

She raised her head and looked at the back of the redheaded girl standing next to her.

"Gee, Ricky," said Donna, "it gives me a funny feeling when I realize that's the last time I'll be saying those numbers. I'll bet I know them even better than I know my name."

Redheaded Ricky West, who was called Fredericka only by her mother, turned around with a look of disgust on her freckled face.

"I don't know why I always wait till the very last day of school to clean out the junk that accumulates all year. After

9

two whole years at Summerfield Junior High, you'd think I'd know better." She surveyed the pile of old test papers, workbooks, and other objects accumulated in her locker with dismay.

The two girls stood in the almost deserted locker room. The room, with its rows and rows of tall olive-green lockers, had an empty, hollow sound. Gone was the medley of voices, raised in conversation, song, quarreling, and gaiety, that was customary.

"Don't just stand there," said Donna impatiently. "If we don't hurry, we'll never get down to the office in time to turn in our locks and get our money back. Come on, I'll help you."

The girls took one armload after another over to the large trash can which stood in a corner.

"Finally!" said Ricky, wiping her hands with a piece of tissue, and handing it to Donna. "Gee, what am I going to do without you all summer!"

A look almost of fear crossed Donna's face. "I don't want to talk about it." Then she tossed her head. "Let's dash," she continued brightly. "I'd really be in trouble if I appeared at home without the dollar we're supposed to get back for the locks."

Down two flights of stairs flew the girls. They pulled up short in front of the glass door which had "Principal's Office" printed on it.

"Now be dignified," whispered Donna. "Mr. Greer always complains that girls today don't act like ladies."

Ricky straightened her skirt, pulled down her blouse, and pushed open the door.

"Good afternoon, Miss Sylvern," she said to the woman behind the counter, who was busily typing.

Miss Sylvern looked up and smiled questioningly.

"We'd like to return our combination locks, and get back the money we paid at the beginning of the year," explained Donna. "I do hope we're not too late."

Still silent, Miss Sylvern reached into a desk drawer, took out a green cash box, withdrew two dollar bills, and handed one to each girl.

The girls thanked her and tiptoed out into the hall.

"Gee, she give me the creeps," Ricky whispered as they walked along.

"We don't have to whisper now," replied Donna. Then she shook her head. "No, it's just that she never wastes words. I've heard Mr. Greer say that Miss Sylvern is a wonderful secretary, and it's such a relief to have a woman around who doesn't jabber constantly."

The girls continued down the hall, and passed several sets of large double doors. Suddenly Ricky stopped.

"Let's peek into the auditorium," she said to Donna. "It's all ready for the graduation tonight, and I'll bet it's beautiful."

Donna paused to consider. "Well, just for a second," she said. "I guess that isn't doing anything wrong."

They opened the door a crack.

"Look at the seats on the stage. They reach almost to the ceiling, like a grandstand," said Ricky in awe.

"And just look at those palms, and the vases of red roses," breathed Donna. "To think that one year from now, we'll be up there!"

"What are you doing?" asked a gruff voice behind them. Both girls jumped, and turned around guiltily.

They were surrounded by a group of giggling girls their own age.

"Ooh, you scared me," sighed Donna. "I thought you were Mr. Greer."

"That's Anne's idea of a joke," said one of the girls. "Come on, let's get out of here. I don't want to stay in school one second more than is absolutely necessary."

Laughing and talking, the girls strolled to one of the large doors leading to the street.

"We all go different ways," said Anne. "So I guess this is good-by for now. Will you all be swimming at our very select Summerfield Public Pool next week?"

The swimming pool, which was open to all residents of Summerfield, was usually the gathering place for teenagers during the vacation months.

Most of the girls nodded in response to Anne's question.

"No," said Donna slowly. "I won't. I thought you knew that I was going to be away all summer."

Anne looked surprised. "Why, Donna, you look like you're going to spend your vacation in a funeral home. What's the matter?"

Ricky broke in. "She's going to be a junior counsellor at a camp near Byersville."

Anne looked relieved. "But that's only about twenty miles from here. Why so sad? Are you afraid of being homesick?"

"It's not that," replied Donna. "After all, I've been away from home before, to Grandma's and even to camp for a month. But this time, besides taking care of myself, I'll have four little children to take care of, too. And I don't mind telling you I'm a little scared."

The girls looked sympathetic.

"You'll be terrific," said one.

"You're used to taking care of kids. After your little brother Jimmy, it'll be a cinch," said another.

"You'll have a wonderful time. I wish I were going away for the summer," said a third girl.

Donna looked a little brighter.

"And it's a wonderful way to earn money," added Anne.

"Not a cent!" replied Donna. "After all, I haven't had any experience. And I am a little young. But if I do well this time and I'm asked to come back next summer, I'll be paid. Mother thought it would be a good opportunity for me to be out in the country, and to learn something too. I hear the camp is beautiful."

After more good-bys, the girls walked off. Ricky and Donna went down the three stone steps together.

"I'll walk you part way home," said Ricky. "I guess you could still stand some cheering up."

Donna smiled gratefully at her friend.

"Look over there," Ricky whispered, directing Donna's gaze across the street. "If it isn't Richard White, president of the graduating class of our beloved Junior High. What happened to all the loyal classmates who usually surround him, waiting hopefully for a smile from the royal lips?"

Donna looked uncomfortable. "Oh, Ricky, you shouldn't talk that way. He can't help it if he's president, and smart and good-looking, too. People just naturally like him."

"Not I!" retorted Ricky, with vehemence. The girls waited for a traffic light to change, and Ricky glanced over her shoulder. "He's crossing the street. Here he comes now. We'll just ignore him."

"Don't be silly," said Donna, a little out of patience. "He doesn't know us from a bowl of beans anyhow."

They crossed the street. Donna returned to the original subject of the conversation as though Richard White had never been mentioned.

"I hope the girls are right. I don't like to tell Mother I'm scared, because then maybe she'll say I can't go. And I know that it really will be good experience for me."

"You know that for my own sake I'd much rather you stayed home this summer," argued Ricky. "We've had such good times every other vacation, and it just won't be the same without you. But I've got to admit I think your mother's right. And I'm sure she'll help you. After all, she was a teacher, and she must know a lot of things you can do with your four little angels at camp, too. You've got to stop acting as though Byersville were at the other end of the world."

"Wait a minute, there," said a boy's voice behind them. "I didn't mean to eavesdrop, but did I hear something about Byersville?"

The girls stopped and turned around. Richard was a few paces behind them. Ricky looked annoyed. "We can't be rude," whispered Donna, hoping that Richard wouldn't hear her.

If he did, he made no sign.

"What's this about Byersville?" he continued. "If you know anyone who lives there, I'd be delighted to look him up. I'll be there for the next two months."

Now it was the girls' turn to look surprised.

"You will?" asked Donna in astonishment. "Why, I will, too. At a camp about two miles from the town."

"This is really a coincidence. You're not by any chance going to be a junior counsellor, are you?" asked Richard.

"Oh, no!" breathed Ricky. "The long arm of Fate reaching out again. Yes, she is."

"But that's practically impossible," said the boy. "I understood it was an all-boys' camp."

By now all three had dazed expressions.

Donna ran her hand through her dark hair.

"There's something wrong. My impression was that it was a converted farmhouse that had been turned into a small camp."

"Now wait a minute." Richard shifted his books to his other hip. "Let's get to the bottom of this. Tell me what you know about your camp, where it is and who runs it and all that sort of business."

Donna took a deep breath. "It's two miles away from Byersville, on the Summerfield side. It's run by Doctor Duval—you know, the famous baby doctor—I think he's called a pediatrician. And the name of the place is Camp Cherrydale."

By the end of her recital, Richard was wearing a broad smile.

"Almost, but not quite. My camp is on the other side of Byersville, it's for boys from six to twelve, and the name is Camp Three Pines. But I've heard a lot about your place—it's got quite a reputation. Incidentally, I don't even know your name."

The girls introduced themselves. Donna noticed that Ricky's reserve was beginning to vanish before Richard's cordial manner. He had a wonderful smile.

"Anyhow, it's nice to know that somebody from the same town will be near. I'll probably see you around. Maybe you could even get your doctor to let a bunch of us boys come over and visit your place. I'm always interested in seeing how the other half lives. Our camp is pretty rugged, I hear."

"I'm sure Cherrydale isn't that fancy," retorted Donna. "But it would be nice if you came over. Why don't you call as soon as the season gets under way, and I'll ask Doctor Duval to set a definite time?"

"Will do," answered Richard, as they came to a side street. "Nice meeting you, girls. I'll call as soon as I get a chance, Donna. And I'm sure of one thing. If the things I've heard about your camp are true, you're going to have a *very* exciting summer." He winked soberly, waved goodby, and turned down the side street.

"I'd better get home, too," said Ricky after Richard had gone. "But I'll see you before you leave. Remember—smile, gal, smile."

Donna lifted her chin. "Somehow, I do feel better about the whole thing now. I guess it's because I have something to look forward to."

The girls separated. Donna hummed a tune to herself. Suddenly she stopped.

"I wonder what he meant?" she mused. "A very exciting summer! What could he have heard about Camp Cherrydale?"

CHAPTER 2   *A Surprise Camper*

The sun streamed through Donna's bedroom window a few days later, but there were no signs of life in the room.

Suddenly the bed heaved, and a tousle-haired girl sat bolt upright among the tangled covers. She focused one half-closed eye upon the clock on the bedtable, and landed with both feet on the floor.

"Ten o'clock!" she said aloud. "I just knew I'd oversleep this morning, and I have so much to do."

"Is that you, Donna?" called a woman's voice from downstairs.

"Yeeks, Mother," answered Donna, through a faceful of soapsuds. "How come you let me sleep so late this morning? You're the one who always makes sure we're down to breakfast with Daddy, summer and winter."

There was a sound of footsteps on the stairs, and Mrs.

21

Parker stood in the doorway of her daughter's room.

"Well, you see," she explained, "I thought that since you're going to be a hard-working career-girl all summer, I'd let you have one day of real luxury."

Donna scurried around the room, pulling out bureau drawers, climbing into dungarees and a shirt, and slipping into an old pair of loafers.

"Oh, yes," her mother continued. "Ricky West has already called to say she's on the way over to help you pack. She'll be here any minute."

Donna looked reprovingly at her mother. "Much as I like sleeping late, Mommy, you really shouldn't have let me do it. Now Ricky'll be here before I even eat my breakfast. Just this once, can't I have just a glass of milk?"

Mrs. Parker answered with the weary manner of someone who has said the same thing every morning for a number of years.

"You know the answer as well as I do, Donna. Orange juice, egg, toast and butter, and milk. And don't forget your vitamins."

Donna started to coax, then changed her mind. It was really not worth wasting the time; her mother always won these little morning arguments.

"I'd better rush like mad," she mumbled, taking the stairs two at a time.

A few minutes later there was a knock on the back door.

"Come in," called Donna, wolfing down the last bite of toast, and gulping half a glass of milk.

"Hi!" Ricky answered, pulling the screen door shut behind her, and helping herself to a chair at the breakfast table. "We are a sleepyhead this morning, aren't we?"

Donna shrugged her shoulders. The explanation was too involved.

"Let's go upstairs," she said, piling the dishes in the sink. "Wait'll I show you what Mother made for me."

In one corner of Donna's room stood a small trunk, and on top of it were piles of clothes ready to be packed.

"Jeepers!" murmured Ricky. "Did your mother make all those things for you?"

With the glow of a bride showing her trousseau, Donna pointed to each pile.

"Over here are the shorts, and here are slacks. These are halters and shirts and these are pajamas. Of course, we had to buy bathing suits and underwear and socks."

"It must be wonderful to have a mother who can sew," said Ricky. "Gosh, you couldn't begin to buy things like these at the stores in Summerfield, even if you could spend all the money you wanted to."

Donna nodded. "I know. We shopped first, and Mother kept saying, 'Why this is ridiculous. I could make clothes much better than these, even on Grandma's old treadle sewing machine.' So she did."

Ricky looked puzzled. "What's a treadle sewing machine?"

"Oh, you know. That's the kind they had before there were electric machines. You have to make them go by pushing a foot-pedal on the floor back and forth." There was a faraway look in Donna's eyes. "Some day I'll have enough money to buy Mother an electric sewing machine. It would be much easier for her to use, and she wouldn't get so worn out when she sews. This one is practically falling apart."

"And think of all the beautiful clothes you could have then!" finished Ricky.

Donna looked at her friend, as though to say that she hadn't been thinking of that at all.

"Donna, will you come here and try on this beach coat once more?" called Mrs. Parker just then.

Ricky watched while Donna's mother patiently adjusted

sleeve lengths and placed pockets on the white robe.

"There!" Mrs. Parker said through a mouthful of pins. "I think I can finish that before lunch. But, Donna, I must have a large spool of white thread, number sixty. Will you please run down to Gordon's and get it for me? I'm sure Ricky won't mind waiting a few minutes."

"Oh, I'll go, too," interrupted Ricky. Then she hesitated. "Is that all right?" she finished.

"Sure thing," said Donna. "It won't take long. Then you can help me pack."

Outside, the warm sunlight splashed on the sidewalk in patterns through the leaves. A gentle breeze scarcely stirred the branches of the old elm trees bordering the street. It was not a day for hurrying.

Ricky picked up a stick and rattled it along a picket fence as they walked by. Donna seemed lost in thought.

"If I had a penny, I'd give it to you for your thoughts," said Ricky after a few minutes of silence.

"I was just wondering," answered Donna, "which group I'll have."

Ricky looked at her questioningly. "What *are* you talking about?"

"I guess I really haven't told you too much about it—

Cherrydale, I mean," replied Donna. "There are four groups of children, and I don't know which ones I'll be with."

Ricky was still puzzled. "Why four groups?"

"The little boys and little girls are two groups, and the older boys and older girls are the other two. The younger groups are four to five years old, and the older six to eight. I wouldn't worry so much if I were sure of being with the seven and eight-year-olds. I've taken care of Jimmy when Mother's busy, and I'm used to that age. But what would I do with the four-year-olds?"

"I guess you're right." A frown appeared on Ricky's forehead. "Gee, I bet they can't even dress themselves, or feed themselves, or anything. Would you have to do all that?"

Now it was Donna's turn to smile. "It won't be as bad as all that. After all, I'm only the *junior* counsellor. There'll be a senior counsellor, too, and I'm only supposed to help her."

The girls stopped in front of a store which said "Gordon's Dry Goods" on the window. Beneath the legend, the window was filled with bolts of yard goods, bath towels, curtains, and tablecloths. In one corner of the window was a small sign, on which the words "Girl Wanted" appeared.

Ricky nudged her companion. "Just what I've been looking for," she said. "You may not be the only one with a job this summer."

The bell tinkled as they opened the door. Inside, the store was dark and a little musty. It had a feeling of not quite keeping up with the times, as though nothing had been changed for the past fifty years.

"Good morning, young ladies," said a little white-haired man who came out from a small room behind the store. "What can I do for you?"

Donna delivered her mother's message to Mr. Gordon. Then she whispered to Ricky, "Go on. I thought you wanted to ask for something, too."

Ricky stammered, then drew a deep breath and said in a rush, "I saw your sign in the window, Mr. Gordon. I'd like that job."

Mr. Gordon smiled and looked Ricky over carefully. "A mite young to be working, ain'tcha?"

"Oh, no, Mr. Gordon, I mean, yes, Mr. Gordon, but I'd like to work during vacation. That is, I'd have to get my mother's permission, but I'm sure it would be all right."

"Wal, now, I dunno." Mr. Gordon considered. "Of course, I only want someone to fold things and put them away. Gittin' a little stiff in m' joints these days. Hard for me to go up and down that there little stepladder. Need somebody young and a-gile."

He paused and peered at Ricky again. "Tell you what. You ask your mother, and then we'll discuss this again." With great courtliness, the old man bowed them out of the store.

Ricky hugged Donna and danced down the street. "Gee, I was scared. Were you that scared when Doctor Duval interviewed you?" Without waiting for an answer, she rushed on. "Do you think he'll really take me? Wouldn't that be terrif?"

"Hold on, hold on," said Donna. "You're not hired yet." Then, looking at her friend's face, she added hastily, "But I'm sure you will be."

Just then Ricky, before Donna's unbelieving eyes, sprawled face down on the sidewalk.

Donna was panic-stricken. Just a split second before, they had been talking gaily. Now here was Ricky, in front of her, not moving at all.

"Ricky," she cried. "Good heavens, what's happened?"

Ricky rolled over on her back, her face a fiery red, each freckle standing out separately.

"What happened? Are you all right? Tell me, what's the matter." Donna didn't know whether to help Ricky up or force her to lie still.

But in a second, Ricky scrambled to her feet, obviously unhurt.

"I'm so *mad,*" she wailed. "That just makes me so *mad.*" And she pointed to a string stretched across the walk.

Donna looked around, until a motion above her caused her to look up in a nearby tree. There, on the lowest branch, sat a thin, dark-haired girl about seven years old, nearly doubled over with laughter.

Donna was incensed. She pointed a finger at the child and said accusingly, "Did you put that string there? Don't you know that that's a very dangerous thing to do? Someone may get badly hurt, and you'll be responsible."

The girl in the tree screwed up her face. "Naa, naa," she said, in imitation of Donna's tone of voice. Then she went off into peals of laughter again.

Donna turned her back on the child and spoke to Ricky.

"Do you think you can make it back to my house now?" she asked with concern in her voice.

"Sure," replied Ricky, dusting off her dungarees. "Just a scraped hand, and I'm no worse off than I was before. Except my temper. Boy, she's a real pest, isn't she?"

"She certainly is," answered Donna. "Don't you know who she is?"

Ricky shook her head. "Never laid eyes on her before. Lucky me!"

"You don't know how right you are!" Donna exclaimed. "Her name is Nancy Bond, and she's a terror. She's in Jimmy's room at school, because they're both seven years old. You should hear the stories he brings home about her! They're enough to make your hair stand on end."

"Why doesn't somebody tell her mother and father?" queried Ricky. "What she needs is a good hard spanking."

"It wouldn't be worth the time. Her mother thinks she's a little angel child, and she's always worried that she's too thin, or that somebody's taking advantage of her, or something."

By now the girls were back at the Parker house.

Ricky looked at her watch. "Gee, it's almost twelve o'clock. Maybe I ought to go right home now. My mother'll have lunch ready soon."

"Come in for just a few minutes," Donna coaxed. "We

can work fast and finish the packing in no time."

Mrs. Parker was waiting for the thread. "Your father just called from the office," she said to Donna. "He made arrangements to leave work early on Friday, so he'll be able to drive you to camp in the afternoon. We thought that you might like to get there a day early and be settled before the children arrive. Doctor Duval thought it would be a good idea, too."

Donna hugged her mother. "Gee, Mommy, that would be swell. Let's start packing right now, Rick."

At that moment the front door banged shut, and there was a clatter up the stairs.

Donna clapped one hand to her forehead. "Can't he ever learn to close that door quietly?" she said to no one in particular, as her small brother appeared in front of her.

"Wait'll you hear, wait'll you hear!" Jimmy shouted.

"I can't help but hear," she complained, "with you screaming like that in my ear. Although I probably won't be able to hear anything else, because I've certainly got a broken eardrum by now."

"Okay, okay," her brother said, lowering his voice to a more normal tone. "But *you'll* start screaming when you hear. Oh, boy, do I pity you!"

Ricky looked from one to the other.

"What's he talking about?" she asked her friend.

"Most likely nothing at all," said Donna. "He's always like this."

"No sir," cried Jimmy, jumping up and down and trying to get his sister's attention. "Nancy Bond is going to Camp Cherrydale!" he blurted out.

Donna and Ricky stood as though paralyzed. Then Donna broke the silence.

"That's not funny, Jimmy Parker," she said in a scolding tone. "You know I don't appreciate jokes like that."

"It's not supposed to be *funny*," replied Jimmy. "It's *true*. I even asked her mother."

"Yeeks!" breathed Donna.

"Jeepers!" said Ricky.

The two girls walked slowly into Donna's room. They sat down silently on the edge of the bed. Then they looked at each other.

"What next!" said Ricky softly.

"Now I'm really between the devil and the deep," mused Donna. "I take my choice of being with the little children, which I don't think I'd like too much, or the older children, including our friend Nancy. Of course it's not my choice—it's up to Doctor Duval—but I'd like to know where I stand."

The telephone rang with startling clarity. Both girls jumped.

"I'll answer it," called Mrs. Parker from downstairs.

The two girls sat lost in thought.

A minute later Mrs. Parker called up the stairs. "It's for you, Donna. Doctor Duval is on the phone, and he says it's urgent."

CHAPTER 3 *Plans Change*

Donna turned pale. Something must be wrong. Dr. Duval was a very busy man, and he certainly wouldn't call unless something terribly important had happened.

"Don't just stand there." Ricky pushed her forward toward the stairs. "Hurry up. He's waiting."

With a sudden burst of energy, Donna flew down to the phone.

Ricky leaned over the banister and listened.

"Yes, Doctor Duval. . . . No, Doctor Duval. . . . I don't know, Doctor Duval. . . . I'll see what I can do, and I'll call you tomorrow."

Donna hung up the receiver and ran upstairs. She nearly knocked Ricky over, grabbed her by both arms, and danced her around.

Ricky looked at her in astonishment.

"What's up?" she asked. "Why the sudden happiness? What did he say?"

Exhausted, Donna flung herself on a chair. "Oh, Ricky, if you only could!" she said. "Ooh, it would be so wonderful! I wouldn't worry about anything."

"I wish you'd explain yourself. This doesn't make a bit of sense to me," complained Ricky.

"I guess I'd better begin at the beginning. Doctor Duval told me that another junior counsellor he had hired was sick. In fact, she has the measles! Isn't that gruesome? Imagine, the beginning of vacation getting the measles."

"This isn't telling me a thing. What's that got to do with me?"

"You didn't let me finish. Then he said that he didn't have time to begin interviewing girls again, and he asked me if I knew someone who would want to take her place. So of course I thought of you right away. Wouldn't it be marvelous if you really could?"

"Oh, Donna!" Ricky was almost speechless. Then she had a dozen objections. "But I already have a job—almost, that is. And anyhow I wouldn't have any time to get camp clothes. And I don't know whether my mother and father would give me permission to go away. I'm the youngest, you know, and they still think I'm a baby."

Donna overruled all the objections. "You didn't really take the other job yet. And I've got plenty of clothes for the two of us, until your mother gets a chance to buy some for you. And you don't know whether or not you'll get permission to go to camp until you ask."

Ricky stood up with new resolve, her eyes shining.

"I'll go home and ask right this second," she said. "I'll even coax if I have to. And I'll let you know as soon as I do," she called over her shoulder.

Donna went to her mother with the news. "That was all right, wasn't it, Mother? To ask Ricky? I'd feel so much better if she were there, too. You know, I feel closer to her than anyone I've ever known. Sometimes she even knows what I'm thinking."

"I know you like her, Cookie. And I agree that you're very much alike. I guess all girls your age are pretty much the same, but sometimes I almost feel that you two are twins. Well, we'll just have to wait to see what her parents say."

The afternoon dragged on, and every time the phone rang Donna ran to answer it.

"You're getting yourself all upset over nothing," commented Mrs. Parker finally. "I'm sure Mrs. West would want to wait for her husband to come home, to talk it over with him."

It was not until dinner was nearly ready that the long-awaited phone call came. And even then, it was not Ricky who called, but Mrs. West.

"Mother, it's for you," said Donna in a minute. "Ricky's mother wants to talk to you."

"Good evening, Mrs. West," began Mrs. Parker. "Yes, Donna's told me all about it. Yes, I think it would be a fine idea, too."

Donna pulled at her mother's arm. "Is she coming, Mommy?"

"The doctor and his wife run the camp," continued Mrs. Parker. "It's a small place, and I understand the children are given excellent care. The rates are very high, but then if you've heard of Doctor Duval, you know that he has some very wealthy patients."

"What's the answer, Mommy?" whispered Donna. "Can she come?"

Mrs. Parker put her finger to her lips in warning, and continued her conversation.

"I understand he takes between fifteen and twenty chil-

dren each summer. It leaves the parents free to vacation and travel, and they know their children are properly cared for."

"Make her say Yes, Mommy. Please, please."

Again Mrs. Parker motioned Donna to be quiet.

"Any special cases? No, I don't think so." Mrs. Parker seemed puzzled. "Oh, you mean Nancy Bond. No, I'm sure there's nothing really wrong with her. In fact, I think a summer with other children, under careful supervision, will do her a lot of good."

Then Mrs. Parker laughed, in response to something Mrs. West had said. "Yes, it would be wonderful if we could afford to send Jimmy there. I could use a vacation myself."

After a few more words, Mrs. Parker ended the conversation.

"Tell me, Mommy, hurry," begged Donna.

Mrs. Parker smiled. "I'm pretty sure things can be arranged. Yes, I think Ricky will go with you."

Donna hugged everyone in sight.

"Hey, lay off me," Jimmy scowled, pushing her aside.

Donna didn't seem to care. "Oh, Mother, I'm so *happy*. This changes everything! Oh, I know we'll have a perfectly *marvelous* summer. Now I'd better hurry and finish my packing."

Mrs. Parker watched her daughter run up the stairs. She shook her head.

"Gloomy as a grave one minute, and happy as a bird the next," she said aloud. "And she thinks little Jimmy is a problem!"

The next two days flew by. Ricky and her mother purchased a minimum wardrobe. Donna, with Mrs. Parker's permission, lent her one shirt, one halter, a pair of shorts and a pair of slacks, "for the rest of the summer, because I really have more than I need," as Donna put it.

Arrangements were made to have Ricky drive out to camp with the Parkers, since her small amount of baggage could fit in the car along with Donna's steamer trunk.

Friday dawned clear and warm. Although they were not to leave until afternoon, both girls were awake almost at daybreak, and by noon Ricky had called three times, with various requests and messages.

"Gee, you would think they were going to Africa, with all that junk," commented Jimmy, as the pile of tennis rackets, cameras, and other odd objects piled up by the front door.

"Now, now, you know you'll miss your sister," said Mrs. Parker.

Jimmy started to deny this, then changed his mind. "Sometimes I guess she isn't so bad," he admitted begrudgingly.

Both girls were waiting impatiently, when Mr. Parker appeared at two o'clock.

"Hi, Daddy," Donna greeted him. "Come on, let's load the car."

Mr. Parker grinned. "Not in any hurry, are you?"

"He's just an old tease," Donna whispered to her friend. "Just like Jimmy."

But in a few minutes everything was in the car. "Check instruments! Fasten safety belts! We're off!" shrieked Jimmy, as Mr. Parker started the motor.

Donna leaned toward Ricky. "I hope the kids aren't all that loud," she confided. "Imagine having twenty times that noise, all at once!"

The ride to Cherrydale was a pleasant one. Just forty-five minutes later the car turned off the main road to a sleepy little lane. It bounced along for a short distance and stopped in front of a large white farmhouse set a few feet back from the road.

Several dogs ran barking toward the car, and behind them came a short, blond, middle-aged man with a pointed, waxed mustache.

"That's Doctor Duval," pointed Donna.

"Gee, he looks French, with that mustache," commented Ricky. "Is he?"

Mrs. Parker turned around in her seat. "I can't say for sure, but you may be right," she said. "I dimly remember hearing that he and his wife were born in the same town in France, and were brought to this country when they were very small. But I may be wrong."

Mr. Parker got out of the car and shook hands with the doctor.

"Won't you all come in?" Dr. Duval said. "We're very proud of our place, and we'd be happy to show it to you."

Everyone got out and walked toward the house.

"Gee, he didn't even say hello to us," said Ricky forlornly.

"You're too sensitive, Ricky," commented Donna. "He knows we're here."

"Donna, will you run ahead and ask Mrs. Duval to come out? I'd like to introduce your parents to her," called the doctor over his shoulder.

Donna obediently went ahead to open the screen door of the porch which ran along the entire front of the house.

She tried the handle, but the door would not give. She turned it the other way, still with no results.

"I think it's locked," she called back.

"Nonsense," said Dr. Duval, who by this time had reached the porch, too. His tone was sharp. "It's never locked."

CHAPTER 4 *Cherrydale*

"See, you just push the handle in, like this," the doctor continued. The door swung open.

"We're so far away from everyone that we just never bother to lock doors around here," he explained with a smile to Mr. and Mrs. Parker. "Maybe it's a bit careless of us, but nothing has ever happened. And, of course, we have the dogs."

A tall, heavy-set woman with bright blue eyes, her hair worn coronet-fashion around her head, appeared on the porch.

"Good afternoon, everyone," she said warmly. "The dogs are better than a doorbell. You can tell when someone's half a mile away."

"These are the Parkers," said Dr. Duval.

"And Donna Parker and Ricky West," finished Mrs.

Duval, holding out her hands to the two girls. "We do so much appreciate your getting your friend to come, Donna. And I'm sure she'll work out just splendidly. I had a talk with Mrs. West, and I know Ricky must come from a lovely family."

The redhaired girl beamed, her previous disappointment at their welcome forgotten.

"And now I'm sure that my husband has shanghaied you into a tour of the place," she added, smiling.

As she led the way into a cool dark center hall, she continued, "We've only had the farm for five years, and it's the doctor's pride and joy. He's always adding things, or changing things around."

"Do you give up your practice for the entire summer?" Mr. Parker asked the doctor.

"Oh, no. Cherrydale is such a short drive from Summerfield that I can commute easily, by making my office hours a little shorter. I'm here before six o'clock every evening, and I don't have to leave for my office until eight thirty in the morning."

Dr. Duval had led the party into the first room opening off the hall to the left.

"This is my office. All the latest equipment, you'll notice. The children are examined for sore throats and such things every morning, and given a thorough examination once a week. Then, too, I can give them any shots they need while they're here."

Mrs. Parker nodded. "I can understand why parents are so anxious to have their children come here."

Dr. Duval looked pleased, and with a smile still on his lips, led them across the hall. "This is the sitting room. We don't use it very much during the summer, because it's so much nicer to sit on the screened porch. But we do show movies to the children here. And if a parent should happen to want to stay overnight, we convert it into a guest room by opening that sofa bed."

Donna and Ricky looked at each other. They had both picked out the word "movies," and both had the same thought. It might not be so bad here, after all.

Back into the hall they went, past the stairs and into a very large room, the entire upper half of it screened. Under the windows were booths like those in breakfast rooms or candy stores, and in the center of the room were tables and chairs. The entire room resembled a charming restaurant.

"The older children eat at the tables, and the smaller

ones at the booths. We had them made especially for little bodies, and we found it was a great deal quieter than the constant scraping of chairs," the doctor explained.

"Huh!" said Donna, aside to Ricky. "Jimmy's seven, and he still scrapes his chair back and forth."

Then they were led into the kitchen, with its gleaming stoves, two large refrigerators, and huge aluminum kettles.

"The counsellors always come here for a snack before bedtime. We believe that a full stomach has a lot to do with a happy disposition," explained Mrs. Duval.

On the other side of the dining room, and in a wing of its own, was an immense game room. There were a pool table, a ping-pong table, many small tables and chairs, and a piano.

"We use this mostly in rainy weather," Dr. Duval went on. "It's fine for arts and crafts, and all sorts of games. We could go outside from here, and up to the cabins, but if you're interested I'll show you the rest of the house first."

Everyone nodded. They could understand why the doctor was so proud of the place.

At the top of the broad staircase, the hall branched out in two directions. Mrs. Duval led them to the left, where two large bedrooms faced each other.

"This is called the pink room," she continued, "and it is where the younger girls sleep."

To Donna, the room seemed like something she might have dreamed. The walls were a delicate pink. Four dainty white junior beds were lined up against one long wall, each with its own white night table. Along another wall were two full-size beds, painted pink, with fluffy white spreads covering them. Organdy curtains fluttered at four windows, and two large white dressers stood against the remaining wall.

"Ooh, it's dreamy," sighed Donna. "I never thought a camp would look like this."

"Not all of it does," laughed Mrs. Duval. "Wait until you see the little boys' room."

Across the hall was the green room, and there was nothing delicate about it except the soft shade of green on the walls. Four sturdy maple junior beds, two full-size maple spool beds, two large maple chests, and draperies and spreads with cowboy motifs, completed the furnishings. The room was as bright and sunny as the pink room, but it was obviously meant for rugged little boys.

"Gee, you don't have to worry about messing up this room," Ricky commented. "You could really live in it."

Mrs. Duval looked at her shrewdly.

"And over here is the bathroom," she said as she passed the stairs to the other branch of the hall. "But I think you'll find it different from your bathroom at home."

Indeed it was! thought Donna. It was about as large as the bedrooms, and though it contained only one bathtub, there were several toilets, one large sink, and four small sinks in a row.

"I can see that you believe in efficiency," laughed Mrs. Parker. "Sometimes I think we could use four sinks, even with our small family."

At the far end of the hall was the bedroom which Dr. and Mrs. Duval occupied, and near it was a flight of stairs leading up to the attic.

"But you have no other groups of children in the house, do you?" asked Mr. Parker.

"No, indeed," said Dr. Duval. "On the third floor is the infirmary, where we put any children who must be isolated for a day or two, for coughs or running noses or upset stomachs. Of course, if they're really sick, we always send them home."

"The nurse's bedroom is up there, too," added Mrs. Duval, "so she can be near the sick child."

Mr. and Mrs. Parker nodded. They were obviously impressed with the way the camp was run.

Then, with the Duvals in the lead, everyone trooped downstairs, out through the game room and up a short hill to the two cabins.

"The cabins are very much alike," Dr. Duval pointed out. "The older children sleep here—makes them feel it's more like a regular camp. I understand a neighbor of yours will be in this cabin—Nancy Bond. Too bad neither of you girls will be with her."

The girls looked at each other, and silently breathed sighs of relief.

Inside, the cabins reminded Donna of the one in which she had spent a month the previous summer. Army cots, dark blankets, a bathroom enclosed at one end of the room, and shelves for storing things—it really looked like camp.

But the tour was not ended. Although Mrs. Duval protested that they must be tired by now, the doctor insisted on showing everyone the tennis courts, the playground for the younger children, and the new swimming pool.

"You really have quite a large place," commented Mrs. Parker. "How many acres are there?"

"Oh, this is only a small part of it. We own forty acres

all together, including all the land on the other side of the road, and all the woods over there." The doctor waved his hand toward the trees that bordered the playground. "Some day we'll work on the rest of it, but you've seen the interesting parts now."

The Parkers took this to mean that the tour was ended. They thanked the Duvals and walked toward the car. Donna and Ricky followed.

"Say your good-bys now," called Dr. Duval after them. "Then report to my wife, and she'll assign you to your rooms."

"Gee," muttered Ricky, "he acts like he owns us. And I didn't like the way he talked to you when you couldn't open his old screen door."

Donna giggled. "You see too many movies, Rick. Just because a man has a pointed mustache, you think he has to be a villain."

"Just you remember what I said," Ricky glowered. "We'll have to watch that guy."

But Donna could only think that her family was leaving, and that she was now on her own.

The farewells were slightly damp, and even Ricky sniffed several times. The two girls waved until the car was a speck far down the road.

The girls walked slowly back to the farmhouse. Mrs. Duval was waiting for them.

"Your baggage has been sent to your rooms," she informed them. "You may unpack now, and then if you like, you may stroll around the grounds. Supper is served at six o'clock." Then she left.

Donna and Ricky stared at each other. "But she didn't even tell us where we were to go," said Ricky finally.

"Maybe she thought her husband had already told us," said Donna. "He did say we weren't in the cabin with Nancy Bond. Anyhow, there's only one way to find out. Let's see where our baggage is. And I, for one, am keeping my fingers crossed."

Both girls tiptoed up the stairs. Donna peeked into the pink room.

"It's here! It's here! Oh, I'm so glad."

Ricky came rushing in. "Oh, Donna, I'm in the green room, just where I wanted to be. And I'm right across the hall from you. Isn't that wonderful?"

Both girls looked around the room.

"I wonder who the senior counsellors are," said Donna, thoughtfully. "I guess they'll come tomorrow with the children. Let's unpack real fast, so we can go outside. I guess any bureau drawer will do."

Ricky looked at Donna. "Gee, you get used to things easily. You were so scared of being with the little children, and now you act like that was what you wanted all along. And you come up here and unpack, as though you belong here. I guess as much as I want to feel I'm grown up, I still want people to tell me what to do and when to do it."

"Then I'll tell you what to do," Donna laughed. "Right now, unpack your suitcase and get ready to go for a walk."

She gazed out the window for a moment. "You know, I think we're going to have a wonderful summer. Swimming pools, and movies, and game rooms. It may not be exciting, but—" Suddenly she stopped and turned to Ricky.

"But that's just what Richard White said it would be— exciting! Remember?"

"Oh, Donna, there you go again. Stop dreaming. Bet I'll be ready before you!"

In a short time, both girls were ready to go downstairs.

As they reached the bottom of the stairs, Mrs. Duval came out of the sitting room.

"I see you're ready, girls. That's fine. I just wanted to tell you one thing."

Suddenly the entire expression on her face changed. It became stern and cold, and when she spoke her voice was harsh.

"Under no condition—I repeat, under *no condition*—are you ever to go past the playground, or near the woods."

"But we only—" began Ricky.

"No buts," interrupted Mrs. Duval. "Remember, you are absolutely forbidden to go in that direction." She dismissed them with a wave of her hand.

Donna and Ricky walked toward the porch, their minds working busily.

Something certainly was queer. One minute they were treated like adults, and very much on their own. And practically the very next minute, they were treated like babies, and not allowed out of sight.

"Could she possibly have some other reason for not letting us go there?" mused Donna aloud.

"You know," said Ricky. "Richard may have been right. This might turn out to be an exciting summer after all."

CHAPTER 5 *The Children Arrive*

"Get up, sleepyhead."

Someone shook Donna. Then she felt the covers being pulled off her. She opened her eyes in amazement, to find Ricky standing over her.

"Why, I thought I had just fallen asleep. I really slept like a log. And is that bacon I smell?"

Donna sniffed the fresh country air, with the unmistakable odor of food wafted on it.

Ricky's jaw dropped. "Not you, Donna! You mean you really want to eat breakfast? Wait'll your mother hears about this. She'll never believe it!"

"Don't go down without me." Donna's voice was muffled as she pulled a gay cotton dress over her head. In a few minutes, the two girls, looking fresh and cool, were standing at the top of the stairs.

Mrs. Duval appeared from the porch, a bronze dinner gong in her hand.

She called a cheerful good morning to them. "Would one of you like to ring the gong for breakfast? It's really only for the doctor, but he's off someplace."

The dining room was as empty as it had been the night before. Donna and Ricky sat at the table with the doctor and his wife.

"Just wait until you see how different this room looks at noon today," commented Mrs. Duval.

"You mean all the children will be here then?" asked Donna.

"And the counsellors, too," Dr. Duval nodded. "But you two girls are the only ones who haven't been here before, so I thought it a good idea to let you get used to the place first."

"While we're on the subject," Mrs. Duval said, "I think we ought to tell you girls exactly what we expect of you."

Donna and Ricky looked at her attentively.

"You take your orders from your senior counsellors. You are here to help them. Our first concern is for the health and happiness of the children, and not for a single minute is a child to be left alone. Small children are much too likely to have accidents as soon as a back is turned. The senior counsellors will lead the activities, and there is a definite schedule to be followed. But remember, except when you have a definite complaint to bring to me, the senior counsellors are in charge."

Then the subject was changed, and breakfast was soon ended.

The girls were given no duties for the rest of the morning, but the time passed swiftly.

The barking of the dogs warned them that someone was approaching, and they ran to the road.

A large bus bounced to a stop outside the farmhouse, and the sound of children's voices filled the air.

Several girls who seemed of college age got off first, and then helped down so many lively, wriggling children that it was impossible to count them. Everyone ran to greet Dr. and Mrs. Duval, who were standing on the porch steps.

Finally groups were sorted out, and they disappeared in various directions.

"I guess we'd better get to our rooms," said Donna. "I can't wait to see what 'my' children look like."

"And the counsellors, too," added Ricky, as they went up the stairs together.

Donna could hardly believe that this was the peaceful, quiet room in which she had slept. There were suitcases, trunks, and children everywhere.

In the center of the room stood a brown-haired, rosy-cheeked young woman. After a minute she clapped her hands. A sudden silence descended on the room.

"All right, girls, line up and we'll select beds and bureau drawers."

She turned to Donna, who was still standing in the doorway, and held out her hand.

"I'm Beatrice Knight. Everyone calls me Bunny. You must be Donna. Let me introduce you to the children."

Donna immediately liked the warm naturalness of the girl.

"Children, this is Aunt Donna." Aside she whispered, "Everyone around here is an aunt or an uncle. That's the doctor's idea. I guess he thinks the kids respect you more."

Then Bunny brought forward the tallest little girl. "This is Beth. She's five years old, and she's got a big sister named Donna, too."

Beth smiled shyly. She was rather thin, with straight brown hair and enormous brown eyes. "She looks sweet," thought Donna.

HATS

"And this is Carol. She'll be five soon." Carol was even darker than Beth, and her black hair if possible even straighter. "Oh, hello," she said to Donna, but didn't bother to hold out her hand.

Then a very blond child stepped forward. "This is Dianne, and she's a dancer." Donna saw a petite, dainty little girl with blue eyes and a turned-up nose. "She looks like a little Dresden doll," thought Donna.

"And this is Susan. She's the youngest."

"How old are you?" Donna asked the chubby, brown-eyed, smiling little girl.

"I was four last month," Susan answered, "but my mother says I'm big for my age."

Donna tried to hide a smile.

They were all sweet-looking children, but how would she ever learn which was which? She felt a little bewildered.

Then Bunny clapped her hands again. "All right," she said. "Close your eyes and I'll turn you around, so you can choose beds."

It was like blindman's buff to the children, and in very short order all the beds and drawers were assigned.

Donna said softly to Bunny, "That was a wonderful way

to do it. Then they can't possibly complain about what they get."

Bunny shrugged her shoulders. "You'll catch on," she said. "And now, if you'll pardon me, I'm pooped. That bus ride wore me out." She kicked off her shoes and flung herself on the bed next to Donna's.

"Oh, yes," she added. "Get the kids into shorts, and wash them up for lunch, will you? I'll be ready when you are."

Donna started to object, but Bunny had already closed her eyes.

"My goodness," she thought in panic. "How can I ever do all that by myself? I don't even know where to begin."

The four little girls sat on their four little beds and looked at her wide-eyed. She mustn't let them see that she was on the verge of tears, she thought.

She smiled weakly at them. "Now you'll have to help me," she said bravely. "Can you each find your own trunks?"

The children nodded solemnly.

"Then I'll help you open them, and we'll take out shorts and shirts."

The trunks opened easily enough. Donna burrowed

through piles of underwear and socks and bathing suits and finally came up with a shirt and a pair of shorts for each child.

"Now," she said, feeling that she had gotten over the first hurdle, "I'll help you get undressed."

Three little girls busily began undoing buttons and snaps. But the blond child—Donna remembered that her name was Dianne—stood and looked at her.

"I'll help you," Donna offered. "Come over here, honey, and I'll undo the back of your dress."

But Dianne stood still, and a big tear splashed onto her cheek.

"Oh, my goodness," Donna thought, "what have I done now?"

"I can't wear a blue shirt with my green shorts," the child said slowly. "Mamma said so."

Donna tried not to show her relief.

"Just for now you can, dear. Because we're in a hurry. And after lunch, we'll find the right shirt. Won't that be nice?"

Dianne shook her head so hard that her blond curls covered her large blue eyes.

"No," she said in a very definite tone. "Mamma said I

have to wear my white shirt with these shorts."

Donna sighed and gave up. It took her several minutes to find the white shirt. Then Dianne's tears turned to smiles.

"Now I can get dressed," she announced.

Susan pulled at Donna's arm. Then, standing on tiptoe, she whispered in her ear, "Now we have to wash our hands and faces."

Donna patted her head gratefully and herded the four children through the hall to the bathroom.

"Thank goodness it's empty," she thought.

The girls lined up at the washbasins. Then they turned and looked at her, obviously waiting.

"We have no soap," Susan told her.

Donna looked embarrassed. "Why, of course," she answered, trying to keep her voice light. "I'll be back in one minute. You wait right here like good girls."

She dashed back to the pink room, and grabbed her own soap dish. "I hope they haven't splashed water over everything," she thought wildly.

But the children were standing just where she had left them. She handed her soap to Susan.

"We'll take turns using it," she told them.

Again Dianne shook her head. "I'm only allowed to use my own soap, Mamma said."

"Here we go again," Donna thought. "This is getting to be as bad as I feared." But aloud she said, "Well, just this once I guess you can wash your hands with this soap. See, it's a brand-new cake that's just been opened. Doesn't it smell good?"

Dianne nodded, and agreed to use the soap.

"Now let's run back to the bedroom," said Donna gaily.

But again the children merely stood and looked at her. She was learning that this meant trouble.

"Towels," whispered Susan.

Donna looked around, found none, and raced to her room again. "Thank goodness Mother gave me some little hand towels," she thought.

As she herded the children out, she wondered what the laundress would think about finding so many towels in her wash. "But I can't worry about that now," she added to herself.

She heaved a sigh of relief when they got back to the bedroom. "What next?" she wondered wearily.

Just then the dinner gong sounded.

Bunny leaped up. "I'll be with you in a second," she

said, noting that the children were ready, but not saying a word of thanks to Donna.

At the stairs, Ricky was waiting with her four boys. "Aunt Dorothy'll be here in a minute, and then we can go downstairs," she was saying.

There was so much Donna wanted to say to Ricky and so much she wanted to ask her. But with eight children around, she decided to wait, and merely waved in greeting.

The dining room did indeed look different, with every table filled.

Donna and Bunny were assigned to a booth, and Donna found with surprise that each side was long enough to allow three people.

"We sit in the middle," explained Bunny. "That's so we can help cut food, and even feed if necessary. Not exactly relaxing, is it?"

Donna hoped the children would eat well. She kept her fingers crossed.

Amazingly enough, she found herself enjoying the meal. The children were interesting, and she learned a great deal about them. And the food was so delicious that everyone was finished quickly. Everyone, that is, but black-haired Carol.

"Still as slow as last year?" asked Bunny. She sighed. "I

guess she'll have to be fed. I'll take the other three, Donna, and you see what you can do with her. They have to go up for naps now."

"I don't know why she gives me all the dirty work," thought Donna. "She'll just go upstairs and lie down again, I guess."

Then she remembered what Mrs. Duval had said that morning about taking orders from the senior counsellors. "Oh, well, I guess I don't know much about putting kids to bed, either," she admitted, as she put a forkful of mashed potatoes into Carol's mouth.

By nightfall, Donna was completely bewildered by Bunny's behavior. She was charming and friendly, and seemed well able to manage the children. But she left most of the work for Donna to do.

"I even had to wash their socks after they went to bed," complained Donna hotly, when the children were finally asleep and she was able to be alone with Ricky on the porch. "I don't mind helping, but I didn't think I'd have to do everything all by myself."

Ricky was sympathetic. "Gee, I'm awfully sorry, Don. Dorothy Leaming, who's with me, is one swell gal. She shows me how to do everything, and I hardly did a thing today. On the other hand, the boys are terrors!"

Donna nodded. "I guess it's one thing or another. My children are absolutely darling, and it's amazing the way they help."

"Help!" Ricky raised her hands in horror. "Did you notice Charles, the little redheaded one? He's awfully cute, but I sure was mad when he took a tube of toothpaste and squeezed it all over the room."

Donna giggled, in spite of herself.

"And then there are the twins, Freddie and Eddie. One's blond and one's dark, and they don't even look like brothers. They're the ones who kept bouncing their beds against the wall tonight, until they fell asleep from sheer exhaustion."

Then Ricky's tone changed. She turned to Donna suddenly. "But did you see the quiet one? His name is Johnny, and there's something very queer about him. I asked Dorothy about him, but she said it's his first summer here. Do you know, he doesn't talk!"

"Not talk! Oh, I can hardly believe that," argued Donna with disbelief. "He's probably just shy. If he's past four, he must be able to say *something,* unless he isn't normal."

"Oh, there's nothing wrong with the way he acts, except that he's very quiet. And he can dress himself and feed himself and all that. He just hasn't said one single word all day. Dorothy said she'd ask the doctor about him."

A figure appeared in the doorway to the hall. "You girls want your bedtime snack? Kitchen's open," said a tall girl whom Donna recognized as the counsellor for the bigger girls.

"Now there's a girl I feel sorry for," said Ricky as they went inside. "She's got Nancy Bond!"

Roast beef sandwiches and cookies and milk soon made both girls forget all their troubles.

"I'll take a sandwich up to Dorothy," said Ricky as they were ready to leave. "She's on duty upstairs, poor thing."

"What do you mean?" asked Donna, adding some cookies to the refreshments for Dorothy.

"Dorothy told me, but you'll hear soon enough from Mrs. Duval. Remember what she said to us about never leaving the children alone for a minute? Well, it seems we take turns every night sitting up there in the hall between the two bedrooms."

"In the dark?" asked Donna, horrified.

"Oh, Dorothy knows how to make herself comfortable. She's got a flashlight and a book. Anyhow, she said she'd probably spend most of the evening getting the kids quiet.

The first night is usually wild, she said."

Donna's turn for night duty did not come until almost the end of the next week. By that time she was completely used to the routine, and so tired every evening that she was glad to tumble into bed at ten o'clock.

"If I make one more sand pie, or swing one more swing, or tell one more story, or wash one more face, I'm going to scream," she confided to Ricky as she prepared to spend two hours in the hall with her flashlight.

"What we need is a change," decided Ricky. "It's not that I don't like the kids—they really get cuter all the time—but it's the same thing day after day. Even movies tomorrow won't make me happy, if I have to see that Freddie doesn't hit Eddie, and Charles doesn't break a leg."

"We haven't even had a chance to find out why we can't go near the woods. Do you suppose we were just imagining that there was something strange that first day?" Donna wondered aloud.

Ricky shook her head. "But everything seems quiet now, doesn't it? Well, have a good time, slave."

Donna made a face as Ricky tiptoed down the steps, and settled herself where she could see into both bedrooms. Everything was still. Donna yawned, and leaned back against the wall. She was really too tired even to read.

Suddenly she heard her name being whispered and recognized Ricky's voice coming from the stairs.

"Hey Donna! Donna! You're wanted on the telephone. Hurry up. I'll stay here till you're through talking."

At the top of the stairs she nearly collided with Ricky, as she rushed down to the doctor's office.

"Yes, this is Donna," she said slowly, trying to place the voice which had asked the question.

Then she smiled. "Of course I remember. You're at Camp Three Pines. I know you said you'd call, Richard. No, I haven't asked yet. Oh, you and the boys can't come until nine o'clock?" she repeated.

Then she brightened. "Maybe Mrs. Duval will give us a late night. You know, let us stay up late that one time. Can I call you right back and let you know? Thanks."

Donna rushed out of the office and into the kitchen, where she knew she would find Mrs. Duval.

She explained the situation to her rapidly, then waited expectantly for the answer.

Mrs. Duval shook her head. "Not a late night, Donna. I'm sorry, but I must insist that you have a good night's sleep. The days here are very tiring, you know, and we can't run the risk of your getting sick. No, you will have to tell the boys they cannot come."

Donna was very close to tears. It was most unfair. Even her mother let her stay up late once or twice a week.

Then, looking at Donna's disappointed face, Mrs. Duval went on, "But we might be able to work out something. You have to be in bed by ten o'clock, but that still leaves an hour for the boys to visit. Would you agree to that plan?"

Donna nodded, not allowing herself to speak. An hour wasn't much, but it was better than nothing.

"May I call Richard back and ask him if that will be all right?" she asked.

Richard was waiting for her call. She reported to him what Mrs. Duval had said. She waited while Richard consulted with the boys near him, and gave her his answer.

"I know it's not what you expected, Richard," Donna said. "But I'm glad that the boys will come, even though it's for such a short time. We'll see you next week."

She dragged herself up the stairs and told Ricky the whole story.

"That's just what I mean," Ricky said soberly. "Doesn't it seem queer to you that she'd only let the boys come for an hour's visit?"

"But she told me why," said Donna. "She said we need that much sleep."

"That's not what I think," declared Ricky firmly. "I think she just doesn't want those boys snooping around."

CHAPTER 6 *A Disappointment*

Notice to all counsellors: There will be an important
meeting in the game room at eight thirty tonight.
Everyone must attend. Please be prompt.

Donna stood before the bulletin board in the dining
room, and read the notice which had just been posted. How
could Bunny attend, when she was on duty tonight? She
had to talk to her about it immediately.

"Come on, Bethie," she coaxed. "Just a few more swal-
lows and your milk will be all gone."

Nap time was over, and everyone had finished the milk
and cookies which were given out every afternoon. Only
Beth and Donna were left in the dining room.

"Would you like another cookie?" Donna suggested.

Beth nodded shyly. She tried hard to please, Donna realized, but she rebelled when it came to drinking milk. And since Dr. Duval had found that the little girl was underweight, he had insisted that she drink at least a quart a day.

"Sometimes I wonder which is worse," Donna sighed. "Carol's being so slow over her food, or your not liking milk. Hurry up, Bethie, or you'll miss all the fun at the playground with Aunt Bunny and the children."

"I know," whispered Beth tearfully. "I try, Aunt Donna, really I do."

"Of course you do, honey," consoled Donna. "You'll be through in one more second, and then we'll run right out to the swings."

Beth smiled through her tears and in one last valiant effort drained the glass.

Bunny was sitting at the sandbox, listlessly watching Susan, Carol, and Dianne make a little village.

"What can be the matter with her?" wondered Donna. "I know she's smart, and she's wonderful with the children when she wants to be, but she acts as though she just doesn't care what happens."

Then she remembered. "Bunny, guess what was just put on the bulletin board!" And she told her about the meeting.

Bunny did not seem at all excited.

"But if you're on duty, how can you go to the meeting?" puzzled Donna.

"Oh, that. The nurse and the cook and some of the kitchen help take the duties whenever there's a meeting. At least, that's what they've always done before, so I guess it won't be any different this year."

Donna nodded. She should have been able to figure that out for herself.

"Aunt Donna, take us down to see the rabbits near the swimming pool," said Dianne, who had grown tired of playing in the sand.

The other children joined in. "Oh, yes, please do," they begged.

Dr. Duval had recently bought two white rabbits and put their little houses in the shade near the pool. The children loved to watch them nibble at the carrots, and wag their long silky ears.

"While you're down there, will you bring up the dry bathing suits?" called Bunny, who continued to sit lazily on the edge of the sandbox.

"Some day I'm going to come right out and ask what's the matter with her," thought Donna, as she led the four little girls down to the rabbits. "If she's sick, she shouldn't be here, and if she's not, she ought to do her share of the work. I'm surprised that the Duvals haven't said anything to her. They certainly seem to know everything that's going on."

But she forgot her anger while she watched the rabbits.

"Oh, look at the daddy rabbit," cooed Susan. "He wiggles his nose bestest. Here, bunny, bunny."

Then she started to laugh. "I know a joke," she grinned at Donna. Donna smiled down at the chubby child.

"Want to hear it?" Susan continued, and then went off into peals of laughter. "These are bunnies, and we have an Aunt Bunny. I'm going to ask Aunt Bunny if she can wiggle her nose, too."

The children giggled until they rolled on the grass. "Let's call her Aunt Rabbit," suggested Carol, and the group became practically hysterical.

"Oh, dear," thought Donna. "I'd better get them back before they think of anything else. Bunny really might not like this."

"Let's get the bathing suits," Donna called. "We'll race to the summerhouse, and then to the swings."

Off the children went, completely forgetting the rabbits. The wet suits were changed at a small covered shed each day, so that the children would walk back to the house in dry robes. Then the counsellors hung the suits to dry on the lines which were placed there.

After getting the suits, everyone ran back to the playground. Bunny, somehow, seemed in a better mood, and the time until dinner passed quickly.

"Put on your most solemn face for tonight," said Bunny, as they went back to the house to wash up.

"Is something the matter?" asked Donna.

"I'm just teasing," said Bunny, and she flashed a smile at Donna. "The Duvals take this so seriously. I know it's a responsibility, to have twenty children who don't belong to you. But my goodness, there are more important things in the world."

Donna felt that the older girl was about to say more, but suddenly she stopped.

There was no more time to worry about personal problems, and it was soon bedtime for the children.

Ricky was waiting in the hall for Donna. "Gee, our rooms are about three feet apart," she complained, "and except for the evenings, we might be at opposite ends of the earth. Those kids sure keep you stepping, don't they?"

Donna linked her arm through Ricky's, and the two

went down to the game room together.

"It's the first counsellors' meeting I've even been to," confided Donna, as they took their seats at a long table which had been set up near the ping-pong table.

"Me, too," whispered Ricky. They settled back to wait for the other counsellors to arrive.

Soon every chair was filled, and Dr. and Mrs. Duval took their places at opposite ends of the table.

The doctor rapped for order. A complete hush fell over the room.

Dr. Duval consulted a piece of paper in front of him and then looked up.

"There are a number of things which I want to discuss with you. First and foremost, of course, are the children."

Bunny winked at Donna, as much as to say "I told you so."

"We naturally have a complete case history for each child," continued the doctor. "However, for certain reasons, there are times when we feel it best not to tell you too much about the children. We expect every child to be given loving care and affection, and we much prefer not to have you think of them as 'problem' cases."

Donna remembered what her mother had said about

Nancy Bond being treated as a normal child. She had hardly seen her all summer, except at meal times, and she wondered whether the method was having any effect on Nancy's behavior.

"Of course, if you feel that you need some assistance with a child, please feel free to discuss the matter with my wife or me. We will do whatever we can to help you."

Donna happened to look at Ricky, and watched her trying to get Dorothy's attention.

"Johnny?" Ricky framed the word silently.

Her senior counsellor frowned, then shook her head slightly. Ricky relaxed in her chair.

Ricky and Dorothy had become fast friends, although Ricky said sometimes that she still felt like the baby of the family, with Dorothy acting like an older sister. But the boys, even from the little Donna had seen, seemed to be twice as much trouble as her own girls. And Johnny, she felt, really was a problem. He still had not uttered a word! Well, they each had their own troubles.

"—second point," the doctor was saying, and Donna realized that she had been daydreaming. "But perhaps my wife had better discuss that with you."

All heads turned toward the opposite end of the table

as Mrs. Duval began to speak.

"I know that some of you girls feel that we are being unnecessarily strict about your time off and your late nights."

"Oh, dear, she means me," thought Donna in embarrassment, thinking of the boys from Camp Three Pines who were coming the following night. But she noticed several other girls across the table who were flushed and uncomfortable looking.

"Do they think Mrs. Duval is talking about *them?*" she thought in amazement.

"But believe me," the woman went on, "we have very good reasons for our strictness. This type of work requires alert young people, and you must get your full quota of sleep each and every night."

Ricky nudged Donna with her elbow.

"Then, too, it is for your own best interests that we limit your engagements. Very often these dates entail boys whom we do not know, or cars which may or may not be safe. Since we are responsible for you, as well as for the children, we do not like to take any unnecessary risks."

By now almost every girl at the table looked uncomfortable. "Well," thought Donna, "at least I'm not the only one who's had this trouble."

"But we certainly feel that you are all entitled to time off, too." She smiled, and the girls looked at her with interest. "The season is well under way now and the routine is established. So, my husband and I feel that from now on, you may have every other afternoon off, from one- thirty until three-thirty, when the children are resting. You will change off with the other counsellor in your group, and you may do anything you like, so long as you inform us when you leave the grounds."

Donna squeezed Ricky's hand. Now they could have some time together. Maybe they could even do some exploring.

"One other thing about time off. Most of you know about our days off, but I should like to explain it to the new girls. Senior counsellors are allowed one whole day away from camp at some time during the summer, from breakfast until the next morning."

Bunny rapped on the table with her fingertips, then looked up, startled at the noise she had made.

"And junior counsellors will have one day off, too, but will have to be back by bedtime."

Even that was better than nothing, thought Donna.

"As for late nights," Mrs. Duval concluded, "they will be very rare, and only for very good reasons, but we will try to see that you don't miss them too much."

Dr. Duval cleared his throat. "There are just a few other matters that must be discussed," he declared. "How many of you remember the entertainment that was held at the end of last year?"

Everyone but Donna and Ricky raised her hand.

"Then if you'll bear with me, I'll explain it to the new girls. The last Sunday of the season, each group puts on some form of entertainment for the parents. It may be a short play, a dance, a puppet show, or anything you wish. Of course, the children should help plan the activity with you, so that they will feel that they are actually participating.

"The program is held out of doors near the tennis courts, with chairs set out on the lawn for visitors. Afterwards, the group which has the best act is given a party by the rest of the camp. But this year we are adding another inducement."

Everyone looked at Dr. Duval expectantly.

"We realize that the program takes a great deal of additional thought and work on your part. So, besides the party, we will give a cash prize to the counsellors of the winning group, to be divided between them."

There was an immediate babble of voices.

Dr. Duval rapped on the table for quiet.

"The prize will not be large. In fact, I may add that the exact amount has not yet been decided. We feel that a job well done is its own reward. On the other hand, extra work should carry extra compensation. And now—"

He started to rise from his chair. Then he looked at his wife, who seemed to be trying to give him a message with her eyes.

He sat down again. "I am reminded of one last thing," he said, and his voice lowered, although it carried to every corner of the room.

"On no condition is anyone to go near the woods. There is nothing there that would be of any interest to you. Even during your afternoons off, when you are allowed to go up to the main road, you are to stay away from the small road that runs into the wooded portion of this property."

He arose suddenly, and strode out of the room. His wife followed close behind him.

The girls left the table in small groups, but Bunny did not move.

"Will you wait for just a minute, Rick," motioned

Donna. "I want to talk to Bunny."

She went around the table, and said cheerfully, "Come on, Bunny, the kitchen's open now."

Bunny looked up thoughtfully.

Donna laughed. "Don't tell me you're thinking about the prize for the entertainment already!"

"Heavens, no!" replied Bunny. "I don't care a fig for that." She caught Donna's surprised expression. "Look, Donna, you do whatever you want to about the entertainment, and you can have the whole prize. Just leave me out of the entire thing."

"Sure, Bunny, if that's the way you want it," said Donna. But to herself she thought, "Well, her trouble can't be money, because she doesn't even make an attempt to get it when it's offered."

Ricky pulled at her arm. She took Donna aside. "Does *that* convince you?" she whispered. "Now I'm positive there's something strange going on."

"You mean about Bunny?"

"No, silly, I mean about the woods. What do you think it could be? Hidden treasure, or a band of jewel thieves? Or maybe they have a son who's hiding from the police!"

Donna giggled. "There you go again, Rick. Do you

still think Doctor Duval's a villain, too?"

Ricky looked hurt. "You may laugh all you want. I still think there's something very fishy going on around here."

But since both Donna and Ricky were on duty the following nap-time, they had no chance to work on Ricky's hunch the next day.

And after the children were in bed that night, they were much too excited getting ready for the boys from Camp Three Pines to discuss the mysterious way in which the meeting had ended.

Long before nine o'clock, when the visitors were expected, Ricky and Donna were sitting on the porch glider, dressed in their best shirts and shorts. In honor of the occasion, they had even applied careful dabs of lipstick.

"Do you really think it's all right to do this?" Donna had asked, as she stood before the bathroom mirror and made her naturally red lips even redder.

"We've got to," Ricky had insisted, carefully wiping a smudge from her cheek. "Otherwise the boys'll think we're *babies*. I just wish this old stuff didn't feel so funny. My lips feel ten times as heavy as they usually do."

"I hope Mrs. Duval or the doctor doesn't notice," Donna had said, still worrying.

But the evening light soon faded on the porch, and Donna no longer had to worry about her strange appearance. Both girls looked at their watches every few minutes, strained their ears at every sound, and tried to pretend that they were not excited.

"But it's only a little after nine now," said Donna finally after a long silence. "It just seems as though we've been waiting a long time because we were dressed and ready so early."

But by a quarter past nine, Donna began to be upset, too.

"Maybe their clocks were slow," suggested Ricky.

"Or maybe they had trouble getting the boys to sleep," Donna contributed.

By nine thirty, however, both girls had run out of excuses.

"Do you think they were just mad at us," said Ricky, "because they could only stay one hour?"

"Certainly they would call, if they couldn't come," Donna defended them. "At least, I should hope they would," she finished lamely.

At a quarter to ten, both girls gave up.

"We may as well face it," said Ricky, rising and stretch-

ing. "We've just been stood up." Donna rubbed what was left of the lipstick off her face. "Let's get a glass of milk and go to bed," she sighed. "And I'll never talk to those boys again."

The kitchen was ablaze with lights. Dorothy and the counsellors from the cabins were finishing a bowl of potato salad that had been left from supper.

"Well, well, well," said one of the girls. "So the boys never appeared. That's men for you—never trust 'em."

"Don't tease," warned Dorothy. "They're still kids. And you'd be disappointed, too, if it had happened to you."

Donna could understand why Ricky was so fond of her. Everyone finished the food in silence.

"It's just mortifying," Donna whispered, as she and Ricky climbed the stairs. "After all, they asked to come. We didn't ask them!"

"I feel the same way," said Ricky. "How am I ever going to face the girls from school? I wrote to all of them, and told them that the great Richard White was coming to see us. Boys are dreadful creatures."

Donna undressed in the dark, still brooding over the slight to her pride. Bunny was sound asleep already, and anyhow she wouldn't be interested.

Suddenly Donna's thoughts were shattered by the barking of the dogs. Certainly nobody was coming down the road at this time of night!

She ran to the window just as the outdoor light was thrown on by someone downstairs. A small closed truck pulled up to the house.

The porch door banged, and she saw Dr. Duval come running down the steps, and over to the driver of the truck. But she could see what the doctor could not.

The back door of the truck opened, and a boy about her age, in white shorts and a sport shirt, climbed out. After him came another boy, and another, and yet another.

"My goodness, where are they all coming from?" thought Donna in amazement. "It's like that trick at the circus where a tiny car stops in front of you and about twenty clowns come out of it."

Ricky appeared at Donna's side.

"What's going on?" she whispered. "I heard all the racket."

The boys were wandering all over the grounds by the house, and Dr. Duval, who had finally noticed them, was gesticulating wildly.

"Why, they're the boys from Three Pines, of course,"

Donna realized suddenly. "But it's after ten o'clock. Why did they come now?"

"And look," pointed Ricky. "There's Richard talking to the doctor. I didn't recognize him with his hair cut crew style."

Finally the boys piled back into the truck and drove off. Dr. Duval stood near the road until they had disappeared in the distance.

"That's that," said Ricky, with a tone of finality. "I can't imagine what happened, but we'll probably never see them again."

She tiptoed out of the room, and Donna started to climb into her own bed.

Something outside caught her eye. What was out there that didn't belong there?

She went to the window which overlooked the playground. In the distance was the mass of woods.

And through the trees, from the supposedly deserted woods, there shone a light!

As Donna watched, it flickered and went out.

CHAPTER 7   *Hot Weather Problems*

"But didn't you even ask the doctor what happened?" Ricky asked Donna the next afternoon.

The two girls were lying in the shade of a large tree near the swimming pool, which was the coolest spot they could find. A sudden heat wave had descended, and although Donna and Ricky had the afternoon off, they had decided that it was too hot to do anything.

"I've told you a dozen times," Donna answered, wiping her brow. "He was awfully angry about the whole affair, and said he didn't like strange boys wandering all over the place. I knew if I asked him another question, he'd blow up and say they could never come again."

Donna chewed reflectively on a blade of grass.

"Do you think I ought to call the boys, and find out what happened?" she asked her friend.

The redheaded girl sat upright. "I should say not!" she replied. "It's up to them to call you. Don't you dare do it, Donna, or you'll have no pride left!"

Donna rolled over on her back. "What about the light, Rick? I've heard people say that sometimes hot weather makes you see strange things. Do you think it was the heat that caused that light to appear last night?"

"If you want my honest opinion," Ricky said, "I think it all ties in. First our not being allowed to go down the road, and then not letting the boys come for more than an hour, and now the light in the woods. It's another clue in the mystery."

Then she stretched and looked at her watch. "It's almost three thirty. We'd better get back in time to help with the children."

The girls listlessly pulled themselves up off the ground and strolled toward the house.

"I certainly don't look forward to an afternoon on the playground in this weather," said Donna.

"Arts and crafts with my four cowboys won't be any better, I'm sure," said Ricky wryly. "Did I tell you that Eddie got a pair of scissors yesterday, and cut off a big hunk of Freddie's hair before we could stop him? Mrs. Duval had fits, but we told her that the scissors are so dull they can hardly cut paper. I don't know how he did it!"

Bunny was waiting for Donna. "We're having swimming again this afternoon, Donna. Mrs. Duval said that as long as the hot spell continues, we'll probably take the children in twice a day."

"Hurrah!" thought Donna. "That puts an end to playground activities, and arts and crafts, too."

Even at supper, when the dining room was usually cool, the heat was unbearable.

"I don't feel like eating any more," said Carol, pushing her plate away.

"Don't force her to eat today," Bunny told Donna. "I don't blame her for not wanting food."

Even Susan, who usually ate everything that was put before her and asked for second helpings, left most of her plate.

"Don't worry about the food," said Mrs. Duval to the counsellors, as she moved from one table to another to see how the meal was progressing. "Just make sure the children get enough to drink."

"Let's sit under a tree and tell stories," suggested Bunny, as they left the dining room.

"May I put my head in your lap?" Beth asked Donna, as they settled down under the tree where Donna and Ricky had spent the afternoon.

"Me too, me too!" clamored the three other children. Finally, Carol and Dianne agreed to rest on Bunny, and Beth and Susan on Donna.

But Donna had just begun the story of Cinderella when Beth said, "Aunt Donna, my head aches."

"You'd better take her up to the house and have the doctor look at her," said Bunny. Beth had turned slightly green.

Dr. Duval was in his office, and he looked the child over carefully.

"Put her to bed, Donna," he said finally. "Bunny can take care of the other girls. It's just a touch of the heat. See that she keeps cool and quiet, and give her this pill." He handed Donna a small white tablet.

Donna nodded, and led Beth upstairs.

She undressed the child, bathed her face and hands in cool water, and tucked her into bed.

"Sing me a song, Aunt Donna," Beth said sleepily as she settled on her pillow.

"Oh, dear!" thought Donna. "I haven't had much practice singing lullabies. I can just picture Jimmy asking me to sing to him!"

She needn't have worried for in a few minutes the child was sleeping peacefully.

"Ssh!" hushed Donna, when the other children came in a few minutes later. "Bethie's sleeping. Let's be very quiet."

She had to smile to herself, as she noted the way Dianne and Carol and Susan tiptoed about, whispering and motioning, so as not to disturb the sick child.

"They really are cute," she said later to Ricky. "Even though Bunny is so strange sometimes, I have a lot to be thankful for."

"I'll be thankful if it's cooler tomorrow," answered Ricky. "Today was really a corker."

But the next day, although Beth seemed much better, the weather was still hot and sticky, and the sky remained a bright, brassy blue.

By the third day, everyone's temper was getting short. Even the cook's most tempting salads failed to awaken appetites, and almost the entire day was spent near the pool.

On the third day of the hot spell, Donna and Bunny

took the children down to the pool at the end of the rest period.

"I can't think of any more quiet games," said Bunny in despair. "How in the world are we going to entertain these children?"

"I've used my whole supply of stories, too," said Donna. "But Mrs. Duval said they can't stay in the water for more than fifteen minutes at a time. And they certainly can't run around in this heat."

"Aunt Donna, Aunt Donna!" called one of the older girls. "You're wanted in the doctor's office."

"Now what?" thought Donna, as she ran toward the house. Her mind conjured up all sorts of dire possibilities.

Mrs. Duval was waiting for her. "Donna," she began, "Doctor Duval told me how well you took care of Beth last night. I'd like you to go upstairs and help Ricky with the little boys. They've all been affected by the heat. Ricky will tell you what to do, and I'll look in soon."

"Yes, of course," said Donna. "But I wonder where Dorothy is?" she thought. "Certainly they don't need more than two counsellors for four boys."

"Am I glad to see you!" Ricky greeted her. "Even when they're sick, these kids won't stay still."

"Where's Dorothy?" Donna asked.

"Oh, she's upstairs helping the nurse. Several of the older children are sick, too, and Doctor Duval decided it was cooler in the house than in the cabins. This place is beginning to look like a hospital."

Donna and Ricky both were kept very busy the rest of the afternoon getting cool drinks, changing ice caps, adjusting shades, straightening beds, and running endless errands for fretful patients.

"Wow!" said Ricky, when the children had dozed off, and she was able to sink into a chair. "We've been rushing around so much, I haven't had time to think about the heat. What would I have done without you!"

"Of course I'm sorry the children don't feel well," replied Donna. "But I do like taking care of them." She lowered her voice. "That little Johnny is a sweet child, isn't he? He didn't say anything to me, but I could tell how grateful he was when I did things for him, just from the way he looked at me."

Ricky nodded. "He likes you. After a while, you can tell what he's thinking by watching his eyes. But he still hasn't said a word."

Donna looked at him thoughtfully. "Have you learned

anything about him?"

"Something very interesting. Last year he was sick—some sort of sleeping sickness—I forget the real name for it. Anyhow, he was in a coma for a long time, and for a while the doctors didn't think he'd live. When he finally got better, he was like this. His parents have had all sorts of examinations made. Finally they decided a summer at a place like this might do him more good than all the treatments and medicines."

Before the day was over, Donna felt that she had gotten to know Johnny quite well. His eyes constantly followed her about the room.

"He really does seem to like me," she thought. "Wouldn't it be terrific if I could get him to talk, when everyone else has failed?"

For the evening meal, the cook sent trays up to Donna and Ricky.

"If we could eat in peace, this would be fine," commented Ricky, as she got up for the fourth time to get a drink for one of the twins. "I've worked up quite an appetite this afternoon."

"I never would have believed that four children could want so many things at the same time," said Donna, wearily resting on her bed. She was exhausted.

But Bunny apparently felt that Donna had had an easy afternoon, and had left her with the job of taking care of the four girls. At the children's bedtime, her resentment flared into open hostility.

"It must have been nice, sitting in a cool room and having a tray sent up to you," she said to Donna with considerable resentment.

"It certainly wasn't fun, if that's what you mean," retorted Donna. "And it wasn't my idea. Mrs. Duval told me to do it."

Bunny turned away. Not another word passed between the two girls for the rest of the evening.

But at ten o'clock, when Donna was ready to go to sleep, she thought she heard the sound of sobbing from Bunny's bed.

"Bunny?" she whispered. "Are you all right?" When there was no answer, she tiptoed over and touched the older girl on the shoulder. "Is something wrong? Can I help?"

Bunny turned over on her back, and wiped her eyes. "You can't do a thing, kid," she said. "And I'm sorry about this evening. I didn't mean to blow up at you. I'm just upset about something."

"Can't you tell me about it?" asked Donna. "I don't mean to pry, but maybe I can help."

Bunny shook her head. "It's nothing you'd understand. You're too young. But what bothered me most today was that Mrs. Duval bawled me out."

"What about?" asked Donna, astonished.

"Don't pretend you haven't noticed. I know I'm not doing a good job this year, and she knows it, too. She told me that if I didn't co-operate better, and stop giving you all the work, I'd have to leave even though it is the middle of the season. She gave me the whole I'm-so-disappointed-in-you-we-know-you-can-do-better line."

"Do you want to leave?" asked Donna.

Bunny thought for a moment. "I thought I did, but now I'm not sure. Anyhow, she gave me until my day off to change my ways. Well, maybe things'll be straightened out by then," she hinted.

"I wish I knew what she's talking about," thought Donna, as she drifted off to sleep. "I don't see why I'm too young for her to talk to. I'm sure I'll be as glad as she, if this thing ever gets cleared up."

The next day was a little cooler, and moods seemed lighter. Most of the children were well enough to get out

of bed. They were more lively than ever.

"It's beginning to seem more like a camp again, thank goodness," Donna said to Bunny. "I never thought I'd actually be glad to go back to swings and sandboxes, but I am."

And that evening, as she and Ricky sat on the porch with several of the other counsellors, they all commented on how happy they had been to return to a normal routine.

Suddenly the phone in the doctor's office rang loudly. Everyone jumped.

"Probably another parent, to find out how her little darling is bearing up," laughed Dorothy.

"It's for you, Donna," said Mrs. Duval just then, as she came to the doorway leading to the porch.

"If it's those boys from Three Pines, tell them you can only see them after midnight. That'll teach them!" called one of the girls.

"Leave her alone," shushed Dorothy.

"It really doesn't matter," thought Donna, "because I'm sure it's not the boys. Since they haven't called by now, we'll probably never hear from them again."

But much to her surprise, the voice at the other end of the phone was Richard White's.

"Oh," said Donna coldly, "I'm surprised to hear from you."

Richard apologized profusely. "That night was an awful mix-up," he groaned, "and this is the very first chance I've had to get near enough to a phone to call you."

"Really?" said Donna, her pride still hurting. "It wasn't necessary that you call at all. I quite understand."

"But you don't, Donna. Please let me explain," the boy pleaded. "The truck wouldn't start, and we almost didn't get there at all."

"And did it take you one whole hour to fix the truck?" Donna asked.

"No, it only took about ten minutes. That's what I'm trying to tell you."

"But you were over an hour late. Try to explain *that*," Donna demanded triumphantly.

"I can, if you'll give me a chance. Your camp is on daylight saving time, isn't it?" Richard asked.

"Of course. What difference does it make?"

"Well, I know Summerfield is on daylight time, too. And since your doctor goes back and forth, it's probably easier for him to keep Cherrydale on the same time."

"How does that explain things?" Donna asked in a

puzzled tone, trying to make sense from this conversation.

"Have you ever been to Byersville?" That was the town two miles away, just midway between the two camps, Donna remembered. "If you have," he went on, without waiting for an answer, "you know that like a great many little towns, it *doesn't* have daylight saving time. And since we're so close to Byersville, we're on standard time, too."

"Go on," said Donna, realizing that Richard had finished.

"But don't you see? We're not on daylight time, and you are. So when it's nine o'clock to us, it's ten o'clock to you. Believe me, no one was more surprised than we were, when we got to your camp and found that everyone was in bed."

Donna laughed heartily. She could understand now what all the gestures and excitement had been about. Poor boys! The joke was on them after all.

"Oh, Richard, I'm so sorry," she said, trying to suppress her giggles. "Maybe you can come another time. And Richard—" she lowered her voice. "Remember what you said about this being an exciting summer? What did you mean?"

Richard hesitated. "Why do you ask, Donna?"

"Well, the other night I saw a mysterious—" Suddenly

Donna stopped. Shivers ran up and down her spine. She turned around, and there, standing in the doorway, was Mrs. Duval.

"Oh, never mind," Donna said quickly, and hung up.

CHAPTER 8 *The House in the Woods*

"Did I interrupt your conversation?" asked Mrs. Duval, and from her tone Donna had no way of telling whether or not she had heard any of it. "I have just talked to the other girls, and wanted to make sure you weren't missed."

Then Donna noticed that Mrs. Duval had several papers in her hand.

"These are the schedules I've drawn up for days off," the woman continued. "The senior counsellors have first choice, but here is a list of days you and Ricky may choose from. Please tell me what you decide. I think you know that you may leave immediately after breakfast, and that you must be back at half past seven, in time to help put the children to bed."

Donna nodded. Mrs. Duval handed her one of the papers, and seated herself at the desk in the office.

Donna walked toward the porch slowly, her head bent over the sheet of paper.

"What was it all about?" asked Ricky, from her place on the glider.

"About our days off," answered Donna, still looking at the dates Mrs. Duval had listed. Then she raised her head. "Didn't you get one, too?"

"Of course I did, silly," replied Ricky. "I meant what happened about the phone call."

"Oh, that! It really was Richard White after all. And wait'll you hear—" At the thought of what had happened, Donna began to giggle again.

Ricky turned to Dorothy. "Did you ever think she'd be laughing about that night?" she asked in exasperation. "Come on, Don, tell us what he said."

Donna repeated the entire story.

"I should have remembered," said Dorothy at the end, "that Byersville is always one hour behind us in the summer. It simply never occurred to anyone."

"Just think of those poor boys," tittered Ricky. "They probably rushed like mad to get ready to come here, and then the truck broke down. And when they finally arrived and found the whole place dark, I'll bet they just couldn't imagine what had happened."

"I guess they never wanted to see us any more, either," Donna giggled. "It was really nice of Richard to call and explain."

"Did they say anything about coming over again?" asked Ricky. "Or are they afraid something else'll happen this time?"

"I said I'd ask Mrs. Duval," said Donna. "But I haven't had a chance yet."

"Ask Mrs. Duval what?" repeated the doctor's wife, who had come out of the office.

"Gee," whispered Ricky, "they sure do hear everything that's going on, don't they?"

Donna walked toward the door leading to the hall, where Mrs. Duval was standing.

"The boys from Camp Three Pines called to apologize for what happened the other night," she began, "and they wondered if they could come some other time."

Mrs. Duval listened to the explanation. "I'm sure it would be all right to ask them to come one night next week, under the same conditions," agreed Mrs. Duval. "Let me know which evening you and Ricky have off, and then you may call them."

"Well, that's settled." Donna breathed a sigh of relief as she slid onto the glider next to Ricky. "Now let's settle the next problem." She pointed to the paper which she was still holding.

"You and I can't take the same day off," said Ricky, "but you can have first choice, Donna."

"Thanks, Rick," answered Donna. "I really do miss my family, even though I get a letter from them almost every day."

"I do, too," said Ricky wistfully. "Of course I'm glad I came to Cherrydale, but it'll be awfully nice to see Mother and Dad again. With the camp so close to Summerfield, I thought they would be able to drive out here much more often. But there's so little time left after the children are in bed, that I guess it's hardly worth it."

"My goodness," said Dorothy, "you kids talk as if you'd been away from your families for years. It's only been a few weeks, you know. What'll happen when you go to college, and don't see them for three or four months at a time?"

The two younger girls looked at each other. College was a long way off.

"Is there any way to get into Summerfield?" asked Donna. "Daddy could never come for me so early in the morning, and I don't want to waste any of that precious day."

"Doctor Duval drives in to the city right after breakfast," suggested one of the other girls. "But sometimes he has to make calls along the way, so there's no guarantee as to when you'd get home."

"I suppose we could get a ride into Byersville, and take a bus from there," said Ricky, "but that would take forever, too."

"Oh, dear," Donna wailed. "One day off, and I'll spend half of it just getting home."

"Wait a minute," said Dorothy slowly. "I think I've got something. Is there anything special you want to do at home, Donna?"

The girl thought for a moment.

"N-No," she said finally. "Just see the folks, I guess. Maybe we'd have a picnic, if Daddy could take some time from the office. I guess I haven't really thought about it much."

Dorothy nodded. "Then how about this? There's a place right outside Byersville where people often go for vacations. It's a large boardinghouse, with lovely grounds. But I know a lot of people from Summerfield who just drive out to spend the day. There's a creek running through the property where you can swim, and picnic grounds, and the boardinghouse serves very nice meals."

Donna clapped her hands. "That would be terrific, Dorothy. Then even if Mother and Daddy did get here a little later, we'd be at Byersville in just a few minutes. And we could spend the entire day there."

"Ooh, Don!" said Ricky. "I think I'll ask my mother and father to do that, too. Let's write to them right now, and ask. We can tell them what day it'll be as soon as we find out."

"I'll get my stationery and the flashlights," agreed Donna. By now the girls were accustomed to using flashlights when writing or reading on the porch at night.

The more the girls thought about the plan, the better it sounded.

The next afternoon they were still talking about it. "But it seems such a long way off," said Ricky. "How will we ever be able to wait until then?"

"It's cooler today," suggested Donna, "and we both have the afternoon off. Let's do some of that exploring we've been talking about for so long."

"You mean the woods?" whispered Ricky. "Gee, I'd love to find out what's going on. But do you think it's wise? There might really be desperate characters hiding there."

"I didn't even mean that," Donna answered. "I thought maybe we'd walk down to the main road, and see what's in that direction. As I recall from our trip here at the beginning of the summer, there's a little roadside refreshment stand. And, oh, how I'd love an ice-cream soda!"

Ricky nodded vigorously. "That's one thing I miss, too. They fill you full of juices and milk and things with vitamins around here. But when it comes to a good old fashioned chocolate soda with two scoops of vanilla ice cream and a big dab of whipped cream on top—"

"Ooh, stop!" groaned Donna. "I'm dying of thirst already. Let's tell Mrs. Duval we're leaving."

In a few minutes, with permission granted, the two girls set out down the dusty road.

After a ten-minute walk, Ricky stopped to lean against a tree trunk.

"It certainly seems longer on foot," she sighed, shaking a pebble out of one shoe. "In the car, it only took a minute to cover all this distance."

"Let's get going," urged Donna, "or we'll never get there and back by half-past three."

As they rounded a turn, Donna pointed. "Look, Rick, those are telephone poles through the trees. So the main road must be right over there."

Suddenly there was a clearing, and before the girls there stretched the highway.

"Wow!" exclaimed Ricky. "Look at those cars shoot past. We'll really have to scoot, to get to the other side."

"Gee, I feel funny," said Donna, glancing down at her bare legs. "Now that we're practically back in civilization, the shorts seem kind of queer, don't they?"

"Nobody'll ever notice," Ricky replied. "Everyone wears shorts these days, even grown women."

The two girls darted across the road as soon as there was a lull in the traffic, and walked along the ditch for several hundred yards.

"Coming to Jake's Coffee House" announced a large sign by the side of the road.

"That must be the place," declared Donna.

"Well, I hope they serve more than coffee," commented Ricky. "I'll be awfully disappointed if I don't get that ice-cream soda."

Jake's Coffee House loomed in front of them. HOT DOGS, HAMBURGERS, PLATTERS, SANDWICHES TO TAKE OUT, ICE CREAM, COLD SODA, said the sign painted on the side of the small white building.

"Keep your fingers crossed," said Ricky as the girls pushed open the swinging door.

Inside there was a long counter. Donna and Ricky climbed up on revolving stools and put their elbows on the counter.

A cheerful young man enveloped in a white apron came over to them.

"And what can I do for youse ladies today?" he asked, wiping his hands on the apron.

"Do you have ice-cream sodas?" asked the girls in unison. Then they giggled.

The man shook his head. "We got hot dogs, hamburgers—"

"We know," interrupted Ricky sadly. "But we did so much want chocolate ice-cream sodas."

"Tell youse what I can do," he offered, looking at the crestfallen faces before him. "How about if'n I put a bottle of soda-pop in a glass, an' put some ice cream in it, an' stir her up all fizzy?" He leaned on the counter and watched their expressions.

Donna and Ricky nodded. "I guess it'll have to do," they agreed.

To their surprise, the sodas were almost as good as the

ones they had dreamed about, and they complimented the man on them. He looked pleased.

"Youse ladies come from around here?" he asked, in a conversational tone.

They nodded, sipping busily through the straws. "Camp Cherrydale," Donna answered. "Do you know where that is?"

"Sure thing," he answered. "That's the doc's place, ain't it? Lots o' times he stops in here fer a cup of coffee, when he's late. Real nice place, too, they say. What you girls doin' 'way out here?"

"Just walking," answered Ricky, who had finished her soda. "Is there any place around here that's interesting? But we have to be back soon."

The good-natured man rocked on his heels. "Lemme see," he thought aloud. Then he snapped his fingers. "Got it!" he said. "You ever heard about the Wishing Rock? It's under a little bridge, near the creek that runs on into Byersville. Around here they say you wish on it, and get anything you want. Ain't far from here, neither."

"How do we get there?" asked Ricky.

The man gave them directions.

"Oh, I see," said Donna. "It'll lead us right back here,

and we can go home the same way we came. Come on, Rick, let's go."

"The first road to the left," recalled Ricky, as they came to a crossroad. "I guess this is it."

The girls crossed the highway again, and followed a dusty, dirt road past several well-kept farmhouses to a crossroad.

"Now he said turn right, and follow the creek to the bridge," said Donna. She looked around. "But I don't see any creek!"

"We followed his directions, though," said Ricky, bewildered. "I don't see what we could have done wrong, do you?"

"Let's go back to that farmhouse we just passed, and ask," suggested Donna.

"Then we'll never have time for anything," countered Ricky. "It's got to be down this way, Don—I'm sure he said the creek was in this direction."

"All we can do is try it," sighed Donna. "I hope you're right."

Soon the narrow road became a path, and the trees grew closer to the road.

"It's almost like a forest," Ricky shuddered. "Look, over

there the trees grow so thick and tall that you can hardly see the sun."

"We'd better ask someone," said Donna. "We don't have much time left."

"Who?" asked Ricky. "There isn't a soul around here."

"We'll ask the very first person we meet," replied Donna. "And I hope someone comes along soon," she added lamely.

The two girls trudged along. "Maybe we'd better go back," said Donna at last. "We just seem to be getting deeper and deeper into the woods. I'll bet nobody has been along this path for years."

"Let's see what's past the next turn," said Ricky. The girls climbed over several rocks and pushed branches out of their way.

"I give up," said Donna, as she scratched her arm on some briers. "We'll just have to explain what happened to Mrs. Duval."

"And then she'll never let us go any place!" Ricky scowled. "Just one more minute, Donna, please."

The sky seemed to grow lighter suddenly. "Look!" cried Ricky. "It's a clearing. And, by gosh, there's a stream over that way. Can you see it?"

"Where?" Donna squinted into the light.

"Right over there, through the trees," Ricky pointed.

"Ricky! Come here, quick!" Donna called as they came closer. "There's a man leaning over a bridge. He looks like he's going to fall right into the water."

"Oh, my goodness!" wailed Ricky. "What'll we do now?"

"Hurry up—we'll have to stop him!"

The two girls ran as fast as they could, stumbling over tree roots and bushes. But they slowed their speed as they reached the rickety wooden bridge.

"He's just standing there," whispered Ricky. "He's looking at the water. It doesn't seem at all as though he's going to fall in."

"I don't know why I thought that," Donna whispered back. "But at least we can ask him if this is the Wishing Rock."

"Not I!" replied Ricky. "He looks queer to me. You ask him." And she pushed the other girl forward.

Donna hesitantly walked up to the man, who did not bother to turn toward her. She noticed that his hair was white and he had a bushy white mustache. His clothes were old, and though not ragged, they looked as though he had slept in them for at least a week.

"He's probably just a tramp," she concluded. "And most likely he doesn't know any more about this neighborhood than we do."

But she stepped forward.

"Pardon me," she said politely. "Could you tell me if this is the Wishing Rock Bridge?"

The man acted as though he had not heard her. Just as she was about to repeat the question, he turned around.

"That way," he said wearily, pointing a finger in the direction from which they had come.

"Oh, dear!" thought Donna. "We just turned too soon." Then, "Why, he speaks with an accent," she thought in surprise. "And he sounds so strange, almost lifeless. I wonder what's the matter with him."

She decided to try again. "Could you tell us the way to Camp Cherrydale?" she asked.

The elderly man suddenly straightened up. He looked at her closely.

"You want Cherrydale?" he asked.

"We work there," answered Donna. "We take care of the children."

"Ah," the man nodded. "The children." He turned

away and leaned against the bridge again.

Donna wondered what to do next. Did he know what she wanted?

Suddenly he looked at her. "Go that way," and he pointed in the opposite direction. "Just a little way." Then he fell silent again.

Donna went back to Ricky. "He said to go this way," she said.

They ran down the road. When the bridge was out of sight, they stopped for breath.

"Gee, he was queer," said Ricky. "What do you think he was doing there?"

"Haven't the faintest idea," answered Donna. "All I want to do is to get back to camp. We only have a few more minutes, and goodness knows where we are."

She took a few steps and suddenly grabbed Ricky's arm.

"Look through the trees," she said. "Right over there."

Ricky peered through the foliage. "Why, it's a house," she gasped. "An old, dilapidated, empty house, and the front windows are covered with boards. It probably hasn't been lived in for years and years. It looks spooky!"

"Do you think it's where that old man is staying?" asked Donna, getting very excited.

Ricky looked thoughtful. "It doesn't look as though anybody is living there. Maybe he just slept there last night. But it's no concern of ours. Let's run!"

The two girls dashed down the road. "It looks—as though—this road—will never end," panted Ricky.

Donna wasted no words, but pointed to a clearing ahead.

"One last dash," she thought, "and we might know where we are."

Into the clearing they ran. And then both girls stopped, and stood stock-still.

"It's the playground!" Ricky said at last. "We're standing right on the road where we were forbidden to go."

"If we go across the playground, and into the house through the game room, maybe no one will see us," suggested Ricky.

The two girls set off. They stayed as close to the wooded area as they could, then made a final dash across the lawn to the game room.

Inside the door they paused for breath.

"I didn't see anybody at the windows," whispered Ricky. "Maybe we're safe."

The two girls tiptoed to the front stairs. But though Donna's feet had slowed down, her mind continued to race.

"If the woods we just came through belong to Doctor Duval, then the house must belong to him, too! And either that old man was trespassing, or the doctor definitely knows he's there!"

CHAPTER 9   *The Boys from Three Pines*

The rest of the afternoon had passed uneventfully. Although both girls had arrived flushed and disheveled, Mrs. Duval had merely said, "Please try to get back a little earlier next time."

"I still don't know whether she saw from which direction we came." Donna answered Ricky's comment after a pause. "But after dinner, when she called us into the office, weren't you scared? I was sure she was going to say something about it then."

Ricky shivered. "My knees were really shaking. And she just wanted to know about our days off. Boy, that was a close call!"

As was usual on the evenings when the girls were not on duty, they were sitting on the porch, talking over the events of the day.

Ricky turned to face her friend. "Now are you convinced that something queer is going on? Doctor Duval said that there was nothing of interest in the woods. And then we find an old boarded-up house that looks as though it hasn't been lived in for some years. Well, that's certainly enough to interest *me.*"

Donna looked at Ricky, her eyes shining. "But of course," she said, clapping her hand to her forehead. "How stupid can I be! That's where the light must have been coming from."

Ricky's mouth made an O. "You're right, Don. Probably only the front windows were covered. If we hadn't been so excited about getting back on time, we would have thought of it immediately. You could see a light from that house, through the trees right into your room. At last we're getting somewhere." The girls fell silent.

"Now we have to find out who turned on the light," Ricky said after a moment.

"And why the Duvals won't let us go near the woods," added Donna.

"They *must* know what's going on," continued Ricky. "And the only person we saw around anywhere was that old man at the bridge."

"But what do you suppose he'd be doing in the house, that the Duvals would want to keep secret? No, I don't think he has anything to do with it." Donna shook her head vehemently. "I think he was just a tramp, wandering through the woods. I'm sure he doesn't have anything to do with the Duvals."

"Do you think maybe he is—crazy?" Ricky asked hesitantly. "Maybe he's the father of Doctor or Mrs. Duval, and they don't want anybody to know about him."

Donna laughed. "Oh, Rick, there you go again. Would a doctor do a thing like that—put his father in a haunted house?"

"Who said it was haunted?" Ricky picked up the word immediately.

"I didn't mean it really *is* haunted," Donna said impatiently. "I just meant it *looks* like it."

Ricky put a finger to her lips. "Ssh. Someone's coming. They'd better not hear us talking."

Bunny poked her head out of the doorway. "You kids just sitting there in the dark moping? Come into the game room. Doctor Duval just got a new game of Monopoly for us."

The two girls arose, and Bunny disappeared. "She seems

happier somehow, doesn't she?" asked Ricky.

"Her day off is next week," answered Donna. "She won't tell me much about it, but I think something's going to happen then."

"Remember," warned Ricky, "not a word about our getting lost. If there really is a mystery, we can solve it ourselves. And if there isn't, they'd just laugh at us for being so suspicious."

The game room lights were on. Several tables had been pushed together, and the girls who were sitting there moved over to make room for Donna and Ricky.

Bunny explained the rules of the game to them, and they were soon very much involved in buying stores and holding mortgages.

"That was exciting," Ricky said, when it was time to end the game. "Let's play tomorrow night again."

"Why, Ricky West!" Donna pushed her chair away from the table. "Have you forgotten that the boys from Three Pines are supposed to come over to see us tomorrow night?"

Ricky made a face. "I'm glad you said 'supposed to.' Goodness knows what'll happen tomorrow night."

"What are you going to do to entertain them, kids?"

asked Bunny, coming in from the kitchen with a piece of chocolate cake.

"Entertain?" repeated Ricky blankly. "Why, we expect them to entertain us."

The other girls howled.

Donna flushed. "We can show them the tennis courts and the swimming pool."

"In the dark?" asked Bunny, smiling.

"We can take flashlights," replied Ricky hotly. "And maybe Doctor Duval will let us put on the outdoor lights for a few minutes."

"It's a shame you can't take them to see the old house in the woods," commented Bunny. "There always used to be a gang of boys poking around that place."

Donna and Ricky were stunned. So Bunny knew about the house! Then the woods hadn't always been forbidden territory.

"A house in the woods?" asked Ricky, pretending innocence. "Is that why we're not allowed to go there?"

"Oh, my!" Bunny wailed. "I guess I'm not supposed to talk about it. But since I've gone this far, you may as well know the rest." She lowered her voice. "But don't tell anyone what I'm going to tell you."

The girls leaned closer. The other counsellors had disappeared into the kitchen.

"A few years ago one of the boys who was always playing around the house fell down the cellar stairs, and was very badly hurt. The Duvals felt responsible, since the house is on their property. They boarded it up and wouldn't let anyone go near it again. It doesn't bother me that we can't go there, though. Nobody has lived there for years, and it was full of spider webs and bats." The girl shuddered.

"But why can't we go into the woods at all?" Donna insisted.

The older girl shrugged. "That's something new this year. I guess they're just being extra careful. But don't worry about it, kids. You're not missing a thing." She sauntered off.

The next day passed quickly.

"No lipstick tonight," said Donna, as the two girls dressed to receive their visitors. "I'll bet that's why we had bad luck last time."

"You're just superstitious, Donna," answered Ricky. "But I guess we'd better not take any chances."

"Ooh, Ricky, I almost forgot!" Donna whirled around.

"I got a letter from Mother and Daddy today. They said they thought the idea of spending the day at Byersville for my time off would be fine. They asked if they could come next week, and Mrs. Duval agreed. So I'll be seeing my family in one more week!"

"Gee, Donna, that'll be wonderful. I wish my folks were coming next week, too," said Ricky a little wistfully. Then she ran a comb through her red hair. "Hurry, Donna. It would really be dreadful if the boys did arrive on time, and we weren't ready."

But the girls were actually a little surprised when just before nine o'clock, a truck drove up which looked familiar to them.

"It's the one we saw from your window, Donna," squealed Ricky, almost sliding off the porch glider in her excitement. "Gee, I never thought they'd really come."

"Ssh," warned Donna. "Now remember, Ricky. We're supposed to be grown-up, so please don't get silly and giggly." She arose majestically and walked down the porch steps with her head held high. Ricky followed.

"Good evening, Richard," Donna said in her most grown-up voice, holding her hand out to the boy who stepped from the front of the truck.

"Hi, Donna. Looks like we finally made it," the boy replied, taking her hand in greeting. "Hi, Ricky."

Then he went to the back of the truck, and flung open the door. "Out, Baked Goods," he called, and out tumbled the other boys. Richard turned to the girls in explanation. "The fellows say that when they're piled in the back of the truck like that they feel like loaves of bread waiting to be delivered. So we call them Baked Goods."

"Sharp, huh?" commented the smallest boy.

"Let me introduce you," said Richard, and the boys grouped themselves near Donna and Ricky.

"The tall thin boy in the back is Ned, and this one is Bud. The fellow with the freckles and the crew cut is Skipper, and that one is Mousey, and that big guy is Early."

Donna and Ricky looked at each other in bewilderment. How would they ever learn which boy belonged to each name? The boys were short and tall, heavy and thin, dark and fair, but to the girls they were just faces.

"Maybe they feel the same way about us," whispered Ricky, from behind her hand. And indeed, though Donna was dark and Ricky redheaded, the two sun-tanned, attractive young girls, both dressed in shirts and shorts, did look strangely alike.

"Will you boys please come up on the porch?" asked Donna. "I'd better tell the doctor you're here."

Several of the boys made faces. "They're not particularly fond of the doctor, after our last visit," explained Richard. "Boy, was he sore! I tried to explain, but he just wouldn't listen."

Donna nodded. "I guess he was afraid you'd wake the children."

She came back from the doctor's office in time to hear the boys say, "Not bad, not bad," approvingly.

"I thought I could show you the grounds, before it gets completely dark," the girl began. "But Doctor Duval says it might be dangerous, since you don't know your way around."

Several of the boys lifted their eyebrows. It was easy to see they were surprised at such caution.

"But I can point out several things to you," Donna went on hurriedly. "Over there are the tennis courts, and that's the children's playground, and way down there near the trees is the swimming pool."

The boys followed her pointing finger.

"Wow! What a layout!" murmured the tall thin boy. Several others merely whistled.

"Just like our old swimming pool, huh, Whitey?" asked the freckled-faced boy.

Donna looked around. Had a Whitey been introduced, too?

Richard saw her expression and smiled. "He means me, Donna. There's another Richard at camp, too. They call me Whitey because of my last name, and so as not to confuse us. Anyhow, most of the boys have nicknames."

He turned to the smallest boy. "Tell her why you're called Mousey."

The lad grinned. "Seems the first night at camp somebody got very funny. Yeah, very funny. Stuck a frog in my bed. I climbed under the covers, and my toe felt something alive, jumping around down there. I could only think of one thing, so I yelled, 'It's a mouse, it's a mouse!' "

The other boys howled in remembrance of the night. "So since then they call me Mousey. But you ask Early how he got his name."

The heavy-set boy turned a deep crimson.

"Go on," cried the other boys. "Tell the girls all about it."

"Well, I always did like to sleep. When they wake me up at six o'clock in the morning out here, I always say,

'Tonight I'm going to bed early.' Only I never do— just keep saying it."

A shy boy who had been standing to one side tapped Richard on the shoulder. "Hey, Whitey, how about Ralph?" he asked.

"Thunder!" exclaimed Mousey. "Is he still in the truck?"

"Gosh, if you don't give him a special invitation, he just stays there," said Richard. He turned to the girls. "None of us have our drivers' licenses yet, so Ralph said he'd bring us over. He's in college, and he's an awful nice guy. He's probably sitting there so engrossed in reading a book he doesn't know where he is."

"Won't you ask him to come in?" asked Donna. "If he doesn't want to stay with us, maybe he'd like to go in the kitchen with the older people."

A minute later, a tall blond young man came up the steps with Richard.

"How do you do," he said to the girls. Then he took Donna aside. "Do you think I could talk to Doctor Duval for a few minutes? I've heard so much about him, and I'm studying medicine—"

"Of course," Donna agreed willingly. "We're going

back to the game room, and I'll take you to the doctor. I think he's in the kitchen."

The boys were impressed with the game room, too. Skipper and Bud wandered around and finally picked up the Ping-pong rackets.

"Mind if we play a game?" they asked.

"More exercise," groaned Early. "These guys wear me out."

At the word "exercise," the other boys immediately formed in a line.

"What's going on?" asked Ricky.

"They're going to show you our morning exercises," explained Richard. "This is what happens every morning before breakfast."

The boys tousled their hair, rumpled their clothes, and put on their sleepiest expressions. Mousey gave the orders.

"Ten-shun!" he commanded.

The boys almost succeeded in standing up straight.

"First exercise, begin! Hup two three four!"

Arms and legs went in all directions, two boys collided with each other, and they all finally fell in a heap on the floor.

The girls giggled until they had no breath left. The boys

were obviously pleased with the results.

"Just a bunch of clowns," commented Richard. "Save the other stuff, guys." Then, facing the girls, "They have a list of gags like that, and they knock themselves out, trying to be funny. Show the ladies you've got brains, too."

Everyone grabbed a chair, sat down, folded his hands, and looked very serious.

Donna did not know what to say.

Then she turned to Richard. "Your driver said he was studying medicine. Maybe he'd be interested in something here. Ricky, tell them about Johnny."

Ricky told them all she knew about the child, who still had not talked. The boys' mock seriousness became real. The talk turned to other interesting children, and the ways in which the two camps were conducted.

"Everything is done for the kids at our place," said Richard earnestly. "There is absolutely nothing done for show."

"Show!" said Donna suddenly. "Why, I'd forgotten all about the prize Doctor Duval told us about at the counsellors' meeting."

The boys were interested. "Maybe we can help you think of an idea for your group," suggested Richard, "since your

senior counsellor isn't going to be of much help."

"Ssh!" cautioned Ricky, but it was Dorothy who appeared at the door of the game room.

"Kitchen's open," she announced, and beat a hasty retreat.

"You mean they just let you go in the kitchen and eat what you want?" The boys were aghast at such generosity.

"Remember, fellas," said Skipper. "There are girls around here. They don't have the delicate appetites you guys have."

Donna saw what he meant when they reached the kitchen, where Ralph was still talking to the doctor. While trying to be polite, the boys nearly knocked each other over to reach the cookie cans.

"Do you suppose they don't get enough to eat?" Ricky whispered to Donna, as she watched their guests wolf down one sandwich after another, and drain the bottles of milk.

"Gee, thanks for everything," the boys said when it was time to leave. They started to pile into the truck.

"Donna, what did you start to ask me on the phone, when you hung up so suddenly?" Richard asked, taking Donna aside for a moment.

Donna looked around to make sure she could not be overheard. "Remember when we met you the last day of school? What did you mean when you said we'd have an exciting summer?"

Richard wrinkled his brow, trying to recall the conversation. "All I know is that this place is supposed to be terribly dull—just the same routine over and over. I guess I was just being sarcastic when I said that. And if I remember, I even winked when I said it."

"You mean you were kidding?" Donna's disappointment showed in her voice. "Well, it is dull, Richard. But it may turn out to be exciting, too." She told him quickly of the deserted house in the woods, and the mysterious light. Richard could offer no solution.

"Let me think about it, though," he said. "And tell me if anything else happens."

He started to climb into the truck. Donna joined Ricky on the porch steps, and they waved good-by to the boys.

"Gee, I guess we really don't appreciate this place," Ricky said to her friend. "Imagine, a swimming hole instead of a pool, and exercises before breakfast, and none of this luscious food. But the boys seemed awfully nice, didn't they?"

Just then the truck door slammed, and Richard came running back.

"I almost forgot. The counsellors are having a square

dance in a couple of weeks, and the boys want to know if you both can come. Will you find out, and let us know?"

He dashed back to the boys without waiting for an answer, and the truck drove off.

CHAPTER 10 *The Day Off*

"Gee, a real dance! I've never been to any but the ones at school. Have you, Donna?" Ricky took Donna's arm, and the two girls walked back into the house.

Donna shook her head. "But that'll have to be a late night, Ricky. What do you think Mrs. Duval will say?"

Ricky sat down on the porch glider, and pulled Donna down beside her. "You know, Donna, I was so excited I forgot that we had to get permission. All I could think of was the dance."

"You're always like that, Ricky. Not that I mind. I guess we sort of balance each other. You always get excited about things, and I always calm you down. Sometimes I think you'd have more fun if I weren't around, though."

Ricky looked hurt. "How can you say such a thing? I wouldn't have any fun at all if you weren't with me, Don.

You're just more cautious than I am."

Donna giggled. "See what I mean? One minute ago, you were excited about the dance. Now look at your long face. Let's figure out how to ask the Duvals for permission, so they can't possibly refuse us."

Ricky rested her chin on her knees. "Gee, I thought my family treated me like a baby, but in some ways it's worse around here. I'll bet if we were home, our mothers would let us go to a little old square dance."

Donna snapped her fingers. "That's it! Richard said the dance wasn't for a couple of weeks, and my family will be here before then. I'll tell Mother and Daddy, and see if they'll talk to the Duvals. Then we'll be able to go."

Ricky gave Donna a tight hug. "Oh, Donna, you always come up with the right answer. I would have just barged in, and everything would have gone wrong. That'll be a perfect way to do it."

Both girls counted the time until the Parkers were to arrive.

"It's not only to ask them about the dance that I want to see my folks, Ricky," commented Donna the night before her day off. "Do you know, I think I've almost forgotten what they look like."

But on the clear, cool morning when the Parkers drove up to the farmhouse, Donna found that the faces of her family were dearly familiar.

"Mother, Daddy!" Donna rushed headlong down the porch steps, and into their arms. "Oh, it's so good to see you again. And look at Jimmy! My, he's grown. Pretty soon he'll be as tall as I am."

Her brother looked uncomfortable but he flushed with pleasure.

"You've done pretty well yourself, honey," commented Mr. Parker, laughing and holding his daughter off at arm's length.

Mrs. Parker nodded in agreement. "You look just fine, dear. You've grown several inches, I think. And you're brown and healthy!"

"The food's wonderful, Mother. Imagine, I even eat a big breakfast now. I guess the country air helps, too. Of course—"

"I know you have a lot to tell us, dear," Mrs. Parker interrupted. "Let's just say a word to Mrs. Duval, and then we can leave."

"Oh, boy!" said Jimmy, bouncing up and down on the back seat of the car, while his parents went indoors. "Mom and Pop say we can go swimming in Byersville, 'n' everything. How about that?"

Donna hugged her brother. "After some of the little monsters I've seen this summer, even you look good to me, Jimmy."

The boy scowled. "Cut out that love stuff. I'm gettin' too big for that. What do you think my gang would say?"

Mrs. Duval came out on the porch with the Parkers, and waved to them as the car drove off.

"She seems like a fine person," commented Donna's mother.

"I guess so," said Donna, trying to keep any feeling out of her voice. "Sometimes she does very queer things, though. Do you know, Mrs. Duval won't let us stay up late, even for dates?"

Mrs. Parker smiled. "She told us about that, Cookie. You've got to admit that if you stayed out till eleven or twelve o'clock, you wouldn't be much good at your work the next day."

"But, Daddy, she'd only let the boys from Three Pines stay for *one hour!*"

"I can understand the way she felt, Donna," Mrs. Parker said. "After all, she didn't know whether they'd be well-behaved or not. Did you have a nice evening?"

Donna told her mother and father about the boys' visit, and ended with their invitation to the square dance.

"I'm sure if we talk to Mrs. Duval, and tell her how important it is to you, she will let you go," said Mrs. Parker reassuringly.

Donna squealed with delight. "Oh, I knew you would help, Mommy."

"And here's the place we're looking for," said Mr. Parker just then, as he turned the car into a long winding driveway. "I think we should first make reservations for dinner at the house, and I'll find out where to change into our bathing suits."

The lockers near the creek were large and clean, and much to Donna's surprise the creek itself looked almost like a clear lake.

"I never thought it would be like this," she said to her mother, gingerly dipping one foot into the cold water. "Near Cherrydale this creek isn't more than a little stream."

Mr. Parker joined them. "I didn't know there was a stream near your camp, Donna."

"Oh, yes, Daddy," the girl replied. "Ricky and I saw it

when—" she was just about to blurt out the story of the mysterious house in the woods— "when we took a walk one afternoon," she finished lamely.

"If I told them about what happened," she thought, "there would be a lot of questioning, and now that I'm away from camp, the whole thing does seem a little silly."

"—and do you like the children?" Mrs. Parker was asking.

"They're sweet, Mother, and much easier to take care of than Ricky's boys. Of course, there's so much face-washing, and feeding, and the same routine over and over, that sometimes I get pretty tired of the whole thing."

"That's what raising children is, dear. When you're a mother yourself, you'll find out that the routine can be fun. I must say, though, that I think the children at the camp get wonderful care."

"You're right, Mommy. I guess we forget it's a job, and expect it to be just a vacation."

"Hey, you gals," called Mr. Parker. "Come out here on the diving board, and join your old man."

"I have been neglecting Daddy," Donna thought, as she ran over to her father and Jimmy.

It was lunchtime almost before they knew it. Mr. Parker

went back to the car, and arrived laden with a large picnic basket and a Thermos jug.

"Mm, that was good." Donna stretched out on the grass a little while later. "I guess I forgot what a good cook you are, Mother."

"Roast beef sandwiches and chocolate cake really don't require any great cooking ability," smiled Mrs. Parker. "But it's nice to hear you say so."

"Mother," Donna said thoughtfully, "when you were a teacher, did your classes put on any entertainments?"

"What do you mean, dear?" asked Mrs. Parker. Donna explained about the program to be held at the end of the summer.

"I haven't done very much about it, because I don't know where to begin," Donna admitted. "Doctor Duval said the children should help plan the activity, and they don't have any ideas, either. Could you help me?"

Mrs. Parker put on what Donna called her "teacherish" expression. "Naturally, five-year-olds can't do too much planning, Donna. I'm sure that Doctor Duval meant that they should feel that they had a part in it, and were not just being told what to do."

"That's right," Donna agreed.

"Then if you have a clear idea in mind, you can lead them as the idea is developed, until you have what you want. They will feel they have planned it themselves. And you may be surprised at the good suggestions they offer."

"Well, now I know a little about *how* to do it, but that's not enough," said Donna unhappily. "I still need an idea. Ricky's group is having a toy band. They're making toy drums and triangles and jingle sticks. But of course she has Dorothy to help her, and Bunny isn't much help to me."

"I've had a feeling that's the way things were going," said Mrs. Parker. "Just try something simple, dear. If I think of anything, I'll write to you."

"Hey, are you two going to sit there and talk all day? I'm ready to go swimming again," called Jimmy.

Donna quickly threw off her somber mood, and dashed into the water. She resolved to think no more about her problems, and spent the rest of the afternoon enjoying her family.

Camp faded into the background, and by dinnertime seemed miles away.

The evening meal was delicious, and the conversation around the table made Donna feel that she had never been away from home.

All too soon it was time to leave for Cherrydale. "It was a beautiful day," said Donna as they drove back. "I think I'm able to face camp again. You get a better view of things when you're away, don't you?"

"Honey, I think you're getting to be quite grown-up," commented her father. "That was a very smart thing you just said."

Donna beamed with pride.

"But don't grow any taller," warned her mother smiling. "I can see already that you're going to need a whole new wardrobe when school begins. And that old treadle sewing machine has gone completely to pieces. I don't know how I'm going to manage without it."

"Gee," thought Donna, "how I'd love to surprise Mother with a new sewing machine. If I could win the prize money at the end of the summer—" her thoughts trailed off as the car came to a stop.

The good-bys were a little less tearful than they had been at the beginning of the season.

"It won't be long now, dear. Be a good girl, and we'll see you soon."

They drove off, and Donna stood a little forlornly on the porch steps.

But she was not alone for more than a minute when a figure rushed out on the steps to greet her.

"Hi, Donna," called Ricky. "I'm so glad you're back. Wait'll I tell you what happened while you were gone!"

CHAPTER 11 *Johnny Disappears*

"Did you learn something about the house in the woods?" Donna asked excitedly, not even stopping to say hello to her friend. "Tell me all about it quickly, Ricky."

"That's not it," said Ricky, calming down considerably. Then she brightened. "But I think you'll like this news anyhow. Doctor Duval announced that we're going to have a campfire tomorrow night. We'll roast hot dogs and marshmallows and sing songs and everything. He's even going to let the little children stay up until after dark."

"Oh, that'll be fun. I guess my family was right. The Duvals aren't so bad after all."

The entire camp was in an uproar the next day.

"Did you hear that the big boys in the cabin are getting dressed like Indians for tonight?" Bunny reported. "You should see them, with lipstick smeared all over their faces,

158

and feathers in their hair. This will be some night!"

But even Bunny had no idea of what the evening held in store for them.

"Will we be able to see the stars tonight?" asked Susan, her eyes as big as saucers, when they were getting ready to leave. "My mother doesn't let me stay up that late at home."

"What's a campfire like?" asked Beth. "Will the whole camp get burned?"

Donna laughed. "No, honey, that's not what a campfire means." She explained the word to the children and told them it would be held some distance from the camp itself.

"In the woods?" asked Dianne. "I don't like to go into the woods."

"Mrs. Duval hasn't told us exactly where it will be. We'll just have to follow the leader," answered Donna. But to herself she thought, "Will they really let us go into the woods? I'd love to see that empty house again, and find out if the old man is still around."

But to Donna's disappointment, the children were led in the opposite direction, along a trail back of the cabins.

"Hold on to your sweaters, girls," she called. They had to walk single file, and Bunny was in front of the four girls, while she was behind them.

"Nothing can possibly happen to the children this way," she said over one shoulder to Ricky, who was leading her little boys. "I wonder how far we'll have to walk."

Though the trail twisted through the trees, up hill and down, it was only a few minutes until the group reached a large circular clearing.

In the middle, logs and brush had been piled high, and a cheery fire was beginning to crackle. Around the edge of the clearing, logs had been piled two and three deep, which made excellent seats and gave everyone a fine view of the fire.

"Come and get it!" called the cook, who was in charge of handing out hot dogs and barbecue forks. Near him, large picnic tables were spread with platters of potato salad, cole slaw, hot rolls, and pitchers of juices and milk.

The children were soon crowding around the fire, while the counsellors showed them how to toast the frankfurters carefully, so that they were an even brown all around.

"Aren't these simply yummy?" Ricky said to Donna as she sank her teeth into a crisp juicy hot dog. "I'm going back and get another as soon as I'm through."

"Don't eat too many," warned Donna. "You can get an awfully bad stomach-ache from too many hot dogs."

Even the children ate with obvious enjoyment. Very few people had room for the marshmallows, though the toasted golden brown morsels looked so delicious that no one could refuse them.

It was nearly dark when the cook threw the last of the paper plates on the fire. Stillness descended on the crowd, as they watched the sparks fly up to the sky.

One of the big boys had brought along his guitar. He took it out, and strummed a tune on it. Soon almost everyone was singing, and the woods resounded with the echo.

Then the boys in Indian costumes arose and formed a circle around the fire. They danced and whooped and yelled in an Indian war dance, while the fire cast shadows on their painted faces.

Suddenly Ricky turned to Donna. "Where's Johnny?" she whispered in panic. "He was beside me just a minute ago."

"Then he must be somewhere around," countered Donna. The two girls searched the faces of everyone around the fire, but Johnny was not in sight.

"We'd better tell Mrs. Duval," said Donna, and the girls walked quietly around to the place where the woman was standing.

Ricky told her what had happened.

Mrs. Duval looked worried, but to the relief of the girls she did not spend time scolding.

"It's getting quite dark," she said, scanning the sky. "I'll get one of the older boys to search the woods in one direction, and I'll take another direction. Ricky, you search this section more carefully, back of the logs and around the picnic tables, but don't alarm the other children. Donna, here is my flashlight. Follow the trail back to camp, and see if perhaps he has gone there."

Quickly she sent each one on her way.

"The first morning we were here, Mrs. Duval said that children get into trouble as soon as your back is turned. But we were right there! How could he have disappeared so quickly?" Donna's thoughts went around and around, as she flashed her light from one side of the trail to the other through the trees.

Suddenly she stopped. A sound that did not belong in the woods reached her ears. It was a child sobbing!

"I'm coming, Johnny, I'm coming!" she called, as she raced along the path. And there in front of her was a huddled little figure, weeping as though his heart would break. She knelt down beside him.

"There, there, dear, we found you." She patted his shaking shoulders, and held him close. "Why did you run away, honey?"

But the boy just gave her a pleading look. "Did something scare you?" Donna asked. A look of fear leaped into the child's eyes. "Was it the Indians around the campfire?" Johnny snuggled close, and his little body shook.

"Now look, honey. They're not real Indians; they're just the big boys from the cabin with lipstick on their faces."

He looked at her with wondering eyes.

"Would you like to be an Indian, too?" she asked. "Let's go back to the children, and I'll ask Aunt Dorothy to let me put lipstick on your face. Then you'll be a wild Indian, and you can make as much noise as any of the big boys. Won't that be fun?"

The sobs slowly subsided, and he put his hand in hers. Together they made their way along the path to the campfire.

Everyone made quite a fuss over them when they arrived, and true to her word, Donna lined Johnny's face with Dorothy's lipstick. When he saw himself in a small pocket mirror, he smiled a little. And with Donna's help, he even put his hand over his mouth to form an Indian war whoop.

A tiny sound came out, a faint imitation of the yells of the bigger boys. He looked at Donna, his eyes shining, and the events of the past few minutes faded with his new happiness. He had finally made a sound!

Donna was thrilled. She had him do it over and over again, to the delight of Dorothy, Ricky, and even the Duvals. And each time the sound became a little stronger and surer.

But he would not let go of Donna's hand for the rest of the evening. While the songs were sung and the stories told, Johnny held tight to his new friend.

"Just one more story," announced Mrs. Duval. "It's getting very late."

"Please let me tell one," begged one of the boys from the cabin. "I have a wonderful story to tell at a campfire."

A silence settled on the crowd as the boy stepped to the center, and everyone leaned forward.

"Once upon a time there was a boy who lived near a forest. Every day the boy would go into the woods to gather nuts or berries to take home for supper. One day he walked farther into the forest than he had ever been before. It was very dark, and he did not know which way to go. Suddenly he saw a light in the distance.

" 'Someone must live there,' he said. 'I'll ask them the way home.'

"But when the boy got to the place where he had seen the light, there was only an old deserted house.

" 'I wonder where the light came from,' he thought. He went to the door and knocked, but there was no answer. He pushed the door open, and it went *crreak, crreak—*"

"Now, now," interrupted Mrs. Duval brusquely. "I don't think that's such a good story to end a campfire. You'd better go back to your place."

The boy looked first startled, then hurt. There was a groan of disappointment from some of the other boys.

Mrs. Duval clapped her hands sharply. "I said that was to be all. Now please rise, and we'll all sing Taps."

Ricky and Donna looked at each other as they stood side by side.

"I know he shouldn't have told a scary story like that to these kids," whispered Ricky. "But she didn't have to use that dreadful tone of voice, did she? That scared me more than the story."

"Apparently she doesn't like stories about empty houses," murmured Donna. "I wonder if she's got another reason for feeling that way."

The sounds of the tender, solemn song rose to the stars. Afterward the hush remained, and silently everyone drifted toward the path home. Johnny still held tightly to Donna's hand.

There was only the sound of footsteps and the rustling of leaves. "At least the evening is ending quietly," thought Donna.

At that precise moment there was a bloodcurdling scream. Everyone jumped, and several children began to cry. Johnny clung to her.

"What happened? What happened?" everyone asked, as they all rushed forward to the place from which the sound had come.

Just behind the cabins a little group had already gathered. Donna could not see what was going on.

She found Ricky quickly. "What's the trouble?" she asked excitedly.

"It's Nancy Bond," Ricky answered. "Something dreadful has happened to her."

CHAPTER 12 *Nancy Bond's Strange Illness*

"Nancy Bond!" said Donna in surprise. "I'd almost forgotten she was here. Why did she scream like that?"

Ricky tried to look over the heads of the people who were huddled in a little circle near the cabins. "Jeepers, Donna," she answered, "Bunny just told me who it was, but I can't see a thing. From the sound of that yell, though, I'd say it was something pretty dreadful. Do you think we can help in any way?"

"No," Donna replied. "I'm sure that the Duvals and the counsellors can manage. Our job is to get these children back into the house and to bed."

The little children were standing a short distance off, their eyes wide, knowing that something strange was going on.

"What's the matter? What happened?" they asked when

168

Ricky and Donna went over to them.

"Not a thing, children. Nancy hurt herself, and she cried," said Donna. To Ricky she whispered, "I hope I'm forgiven for not telling the whole truth."

"Is that all!" said Susan. "I never scream like that, because I'm a big girl now, and only babies cry when they're hurt!"

Donna rumpled the soft brown curls, and smiled at the rosy-cheeked little face.

"Huh!" said Freddie. "I thought one of the Indians shot her with his bow and arrow."

Johnny looked up at Donna questioningly. Donna understood what he wanted to say.

"But they aren't real Indians," she answered. "They're just the big boys dressed up. See, Johnny is an Indian, too, because he's a big boy now."

Johnny smiled a brief smile, and held on to Donna's arm. She felt that she could almost read what was in his mind now.

Bunny and Dorothy joined them, and they all went back to the house.

"Let's get the kids to bed fast," said Bunny. "I've just got to know what happened."

Donna looked at her in surprise. "Why, Bunny, I thought you were over there. I didn't want to question you in front of the children, but I certainly thought you could tell me what was wrong."

"All I saw was Nancy, lying on the ground and moaning and groaning. Doctor Duval was leaning over her, but I couldn't hear anything he said."

"I hope the children remember the nice part of the campfire, and not the end," remarked Donna as she turned off the light in the pink room. Everything was quiet in the house when Ricky met them in the hall.

Then a door slammed, and there was a sound of great confusion below. In a minute a procession appeared on the stairs, and the girls scooted to one side so they would not be in the way.

First came Dr. Duval, looking pale and worried. Behind him came the nurse in her starched white uniform, and Nancy's counsellor. Between them, still moaning, and clutching her abdomen, was Nancy Bond herself. Behind her came Mrs. Duval.

Slowly they climbed the stairs, not even looking at the three girls on the landing. The footsteps continued as they mounted to the third floor infirmary.

"Gee, she really looked sick. She was actually green," commented Donna.

"I don't trust that girl, after what she did to me," said Ricky. "But, boy, she certainly does look sick! I wonder what happened."

"Did you see the way she was holding her side?" added Bunny. "I'll bet she's got appendicitis."

"Would that make her scream?" asked Donna thoughtfully and soberly.

"Well—" Bunny hesitated. "I guess most people wouldn't, but with Nancy it's perfectly possible. Her counsellor says she's improved a great deal since the beginning of the summer, but she can be one big pain in the neck when she wants to."

"Suppose it is appendicitis?" asked Donna. "What could they do?"

"I guess they'd have to rush her to the hospital," replied Bunny.

"Maybe it's too late," said Ricky in a rush of words.

"Maybe it's an emergency, and she can't be moved, and Doctor Duval will have to operate on the kitchen table, with pots of water boiling all around, like they always do in the movies I've seen."

Donna looked at her friend disapprovingly. "Oh, Ricky, you've got to make a big story out of everything, don't you?"

Before Ricky had a chance to answer, the doctor rushed down past them and into his office.

"I guess we won't learn anything for a while," said Bunny, moving away. "See you later." Donna and Ricky followed her down the stairs.

As they reached the bottom, Dr. Duval's voice came clear and loud.

"No, Mrs. Bond," he was saying. "Your daughter is in no immediate danger. It's too soon to tell exactly what is wrong, but I thought I ought to call you. Yes, we'll watch her carefully."

There was a short silence. Then the doctor's voice wearily said, "My dear woman, there is no need to carry on like that. I assure you we are doing everything possible for Nancy. Don't you think you could wait until tomorrow morning to see her?"

Another silence. "Very well," he answered finally. "You may come tonight. We will arrange to have you sleep in the downstairs room."

"Oh, me, oh, my," said Donna to Ricky as they sank

into their usual places on the porch. "When that woman comes, the fun will really begin."

Dr. Duval appeared on the porch. "Do you girls mind if I join you here?" he inquired. "I think I need a little fresh air."

But he had not been sitting there for more than a minute when the nurse appeared.

Dr. Duval looked up inquiringly. He seemed surprised to see her.

"It's all right," Miss Patton assured him. "Mrs. Duval is still upstairs with Nancy, and she seems a little quieter. I thought you ought to know something, however. She just admitted to us that she had six hot dogs, and finished two more that the other girls didn't want. She also had three helpings of potato salad, and about half a pound of marshmallows."

"What!" Doctor Duval shot up into the air. "Why was she allowed to have all that? I gave strict orders that the counsellors were to see that none overate. This is disgraceful!"

"Oh, she was clever about it," replied the nurse. "She made each of the other girls get extra helpings and give them to her. It seems that they're all afraid of her."

"This is dreadful, dreadful," the doctor kept repeating. "We'll have to keep her until she is well, but I will not have a child like this in my camp. If what she has told you is true, she is to leave here the minute she is better." He strode into the house, his face almost purple with rage.

Ricky looked at Donna as though to say "I told you so."

"I wonder if he'll tell Mrs. Bond not to come now," Donna said. "No—" she answered her own question. "If I know that woman, she's halfway here already."

"They must have been going seventy miles an hour all the way," whispered Ricky, as Mr. and Mrs. Bond appeared at the farmhouse a little while later.

Lights were turned on all over the house, for Mrs. Bond insisted on being taken to see her daughter immediately.

"If she wakes those children, I think I'll strangle her," warned Ricky, as Mrs. Bond's voice carried down three floors to them. "Honestly, you'd think no one ever had a stomach-ache before. And it's Nancy's own fault, too!"

"I wonder if she'll stay overnight, since they know it's nothing serious," commented Donna as they were undressing. They could still hear voices from the third floor.

The next morning Mrs. Bond was still there. Moreover, she seemed very much at home.

As Donna came down to breakfast with the children, Mrs. Bond came out of the kitchen.

"Will you please take this juice up to Nancy?" she asked Donna in a wheedling tone, handing her a glass. "There are so many steps for me to walk. And tell her that Mother will be with her precious in just a few little minutes."

Donna stared at her in amazement. Then she shrugged her shoulders and climbed to the third floor.

When she told Ricky about it, Ricky scowled. "Don't I know it! She's had everybody running up and down the stairs all day long. And she's poked her nose into all the pots in the kitchen, until the cook is about ready to go after her with a carving knife. It's no wonder Nancy is the way she is, with a mother like that!"

The girls did not spend too much time worrying about Mrs. Bond and Nancy, however, for more important things were happening.

"I've been meaning to talk to you girls," said Mrs. Duval at suppertime. "Donna, your mother called yesterday just before the campfire and mentioned something about a square dance. If you'd like to go, I think it can be arranged."

Donna and Ricky beamed. They thanked Mrs. Duval

several times for giving her permission.

"You'll have to check with the chart to make sure you're not on duty that night. Then this evening you may call the boys. Of course, they must come for you, and you must be back before midnight."

"Why does she have to be like that?" asked Ricky. "If and if and if. If we're not on duty, and if the boys can come for us, and if we get back at a certain time—"

"Why, Ricky!" Donna was shocked. "I thought you'd be happy just to get a late night. Let's hope the boys still want us to come."

The boys were delighted, and willingly agreed to meet all of Mrs. Duval's demands.

"And we're not on duty, either," Ricky said joyfully, twirling Donna around. "Oh, it's going to be a wonderful night!"

"Whatever are you kids doing?" Dorothy asked during one rest hour when she saw the girls seated on the floor in the pink room. They were pouring over Donna's trunk, and there were piles of clothes all over the floor.

"Donna brought loads and loads of clothes," answered Ricky, "but there isn't a thing we can wear to a square dance."

Dorothy laughed. "That's right. You gals will have to get all dressed up in skirts for the occasion, won't you? Well, let's see what we can find."

She went into the green room and pulled her steamer trunk out from beneath her bed. "There!" she exclaimed, holding up a gaily patterned skirt. "This is about three yards wide, and I think it'll fit one of you."

"Oh, that's darling," said Ricky, holding it up to her waist. "Here, Donna, you ought to wear this. It'll be just perfect with your blouse."

"Just a minute," Dorothy broke in. "I'm sure Bunny must have something you can wear, too. Let's ask her as soon as she comes in."

When Bunny appeared to look for a pencil, all the girls gathered around her. Bunny dug into her trunk and came up with a bright cotton skirt.

"Ooh, that'll be wonderful with your red hair," said Donna. "You girls are real dolls to lend us your things. Aren't they, Ricky?" She danced around with the skirt held in front of her.

"Well, that problem's solved." She heaved a sigh of relief. "Only a few more days to wait. I keep feeling something's going to go wrong."

"Pooh!" said Ricky. "You're just an old worrier. Everything is going to be just wonderful."

When nothing had happened by the day before the dance, Donna began to believe that Ricky was right. Then suddenly Bunny came to her, wearing a troubled, worried expression.

"Donna, I have some awfully bad news for you," she began hesitantly.

"Why, what's the trouble, Bunny?" the younger girl asked. "If you've decided you'd better not lend us the skirt, I'm sure Ricky will understand."

The frown on Bunny's forehead deepened. "I'm afraid it's much more serious than that. I feel it's completely my fault. I knew all along that your dance is in three more days, but it just never clicked until a little while ago."

"I don't understand. The only thing that could stop us from going is for the dance to be called off, or for no one to be here to take care of the children till we got back—" Donna stopped in the middle of her sentence. "You can't mean—"

Bunny nodded and bit her lip. She looked truly upset. "Yes, I do. It's the only night in the whole summer that I won't be here. Oh, Donna, you do understand, don't you?

It's so terribly important that I go home then."

Donna sank into a chair. "I knew it. I just knew it. Everything was too perfect to last." Then she sighed and said bravely, "Of course I understand how you've looked forward to your day off, Bunny. I should have remembered, too. Well, I'd better go and tell Ricky that she'll have to go without me."

But Ricky would have none of it.

"Absolutely, definitely, and positively, no!" she stated when Donna told her the news. "It's your date, Donna. Richard really wanted you, and I'm just tagging along. I simply will not go without you, and that's final. Unless—"

Donna raised her head. "Unless what?"

Ricky rested her chin in the palm of her hand.

"Isn't there someone who could possibly stay with the children until you get back? I know Dorothy would, but Mrs. Duval wouldn't let her stay up till twelve o'clock, and she couldn't sleep in two rooms at the same time."

"You might have something there. Isn't there somebody else who could stay with them?"

The two girls were quiet. Then Ricky let out a little screech. "I've got it! How about Miss Patton?"

"You mean the nurse? But Nancy Bond is still up there

in the infirmary, isn't she?"

"My goodness," said Ricky. "You mean she isn't back at the cabin yet? She could have gotten over a dozen upset stomachs by now."

"But you know her mother—" Donna's voice trailed off. "Well, we could ask Miss Patton anyhow, I guess. If Nancy's practically well, she's certainly able to be left alone for a few hours. It's not as though she were four years old, and likely to wake up in the middle of the night."

At their first free moment, the girls went straight to Miss Patton.

"Of course you girls know that it is entirely up to Mrs. Duval. But you may tell her that I'm perfectly willing to do it." The nurse smiled sweetly at them. Then she leaned forward and whispered, "Frankly, I'd be delighted. I'm just about going mad up here with that child. She's no sicker than I am, and she sleeps like a log every night."

"Isn't she a dear?" Donna asked as they went to find Mrs. Duval. "This may work out after all."

To their surprise, Mrs. Duval offered no objection to the plan.

"We made it! We made it!" The girls hugged each other as they left the doctor's office.

"How will we ever wait till the night of the dance?" Ricky wondered, scarcely able to control her excitement.

The minutes ticked off one by one, until finally the morning of the great day arrived.

"I was sure it was going to rain today." Donna yawned as she threw off the covers and looked at the bright blue sky.

"It could snow today for all I care," said Bunny, tossing things into a suitcase.

Donna looked at her thoughtfully. "I don't know whether to say anything about it, Bunny—but have you decided what to do about camp? You know, about the conversation you and Mrs. Duval had."

Bunny had a far-off look in her eyes. "That's part of it. I'll have to decide today whether or not I want to come back. And if I don't—well, I want you to know how much I appreciate everything you've done."

Donna was close to tears. "I haven't done a thing, Bunny. And I do hope you can come back."

But after Bunny left, Donna was so busy taking complete charge of the four little girls that she had no time to worry about the older girl's problems. In fact, she wondered if she would have the energy to do any square-dancing with the boys at all that evening.

But a cool shower and the excitement of getting dressed soon changed her feeling.

Her eyes were shining as she twirled around in front of the bathroom mirror.

Ricky looked her over carefully, then nodded approvingly. "You look terrific," she said.

"You, too," answered Donna. "But don't these skirts feel funny? After being in shorts all summer, I feel as though I'm wearing a masquerade costume."

"Come on, Don. The truck will be here any minute. It would be dreadful if they started honking the horn."

"I just want to say good night to Miss Patton," said Donna. "I'll be right down."

As she tiptoed down the stairs a few minutes later, she could hear a low murmur of voices coming from the doctor's office.

She passed the open door and arrived on the porch just as the truck pulled up in front of the house.

"Hurry, Donna." Ricky pulled at her arm.

"Wait a minute, Ricky," Donna whispered. "I just heard something amazing."

"Well, hurry up. The boys are waiting." Ricky was impatient to be off.

"I just passed the doctor's office, and I heard Mrs. Duval say 'empty house,' and the next thing I knew, the doctor was saying, 'I wonder how much those two girls have found out'!"

CHAPTER 13 *The Square Dance*

Ricky's eyes opened wide.

"Are you sure that's what he said?" she asked.

Donna nodded solemnly. "Absolutely. But come on— this is no place to talk."

Ricky stood still. "But how do you know he meant us?"

Donna tugged at her friend. "I just do, that's all. Come *on,* Ricky. We'll simply have to wait till we get back to discuss this."

"Oh, dear," wailed Ricky. "That's what always happens. Just when things get exciting, we have to leave. Now I'll be so anxious to get back, that I'm sure I won't enjoy myself."

Donna smiled. She knew how quickly Ricky would forget what she had just said.

"Hey, what are you two girls doing there? It'll be midnight before you even leave this place, if you don't hurry," called Richard, getting out of the truck and coming toward them.

"Good evening, Richard," they called.

"There isn't room for all of us in front, is there?" asked Donna.

"You wouldn't want to sit there even if there were room," laughed Richard. "Those front seats have no springs, and you need cast iron insides to ride up front and come out alive."

He opened the doors at the back of the truck.

"You mean we sit on the—floor?" asked Ricky.

The girls cautiously peered inside. In honor of their guests, the boys had covered the entire floor of the truck with a flowered cloth, and had painted designs on the sides of the truck so that it resembled a weird tropical garden.

"That stuff on the floor is something our cook has been saving for years, to make curtains for the kitchen. But we thought there was a much better use for it." He beamed proudly.

"It's—it's lovely," said Donna at last. "You must have gone to a lot of trouble, just for us."

"Think nothing of it." He helped them inside. "I'll sit

in back with you. Ralph won't mind sitting up front by himself. Will you, old boy?"

The tall blond young man waved in answer. "All set?" he asked, as he got out to close the truck doors, and then climbed back into the driver's seat. "Hang on tight!"

The girls realized that he meant exactly that, as the truck gave a terrific lurch forward.

"Wow!" said Ricky, as she sprawled on the floor. "This thing really has power, hasn't it?"

"Right turn!" called Ralph, and the car careened far over on one side.

"It's a good thing the two camps are only a few miles apart," said Richard as the truck finally slowed down. "Now you can really say you've lived dangerously."

The girls alighted a trifle shakily and smoothed out their skirts and their hair.

"It was a very—*interesting*—ride," said Donna a little nervously. "Do we go back the same way?"

"Sure, sure," said Richard, mistaking her concern for delight. "You know, you two are good sports. There are a lot of girls I know who would refuse to ride in trusty old Betsy." He patted the motor of the truck fondly.

Ricky and Donna smiled weakly at the compliment. "I

hope we make it," whispered Ricky, as Richard led them toward a large log cabin.

"This is our mess hall," he pointed out. "Later on in the evening we'll come down here to eat."

"Where is the dance going to be held?" asked Donna as they passed the building and walked toward a group of smaller cabins.

"In the old barn, just past that hill," answered Richard. "We use the upper part of the barn for a gym, and for our entertainments. These little bunks are where the boys sleep."

The fields through which they walked were uneven, and the grass was rough and several inches high in places.

"Not like the country club lawns at Cherrydale, is it?" asked Richard, as Donna stumbled. "Let's get right over to the barn now, because that's where everyone is. I can show you the rest of the place later."

As they reached the top of the hill, several buildings came into view.

"Which one is the barn?" asked Ricky.

"The tallest one, over there," and Richard pointed to a large stone building with a slanted roof. "Those low buildings over in that direction are still called the farmhouse, but now they're used for meeting rooms, and the infirmary, and the caretaker's quarters. You know, that place was built before George Washington's time."

"You like this camp, don't you?" asked Donna, turning to look at the boy.

"It's a swell place," he agreed. "I'm having the best summer I've ever had. We have country fairs and hikes and a campfire every week. Of course we work hard, too."

They walked up a long flight of stairs on the outside of the barn, and found themselves in a large hall. The floor was of highly polished wood; the ceiling was very high and beamed. And in the crevices of the rough stones which formed the walls, were dozens of candles which cast a flickering light over the whole room.

"Ooh, it looks dreamy," breathed Donna.

"It's—it's so *romantic,*" murmured Ricky.

"You can't imagine how hard we worked," replied Richard matter-of-factly. "This place was a horrible mess this afternoon, with basketball stuff and paint cans and old stage scenery, and all sorts of junk all over the place. And let me tell you, it's no easy job to stick all those candles in the wall. I practically fell off the ladder half a dozen times."

Several boys who looked familiar came toward them.

"You remember these guys, don't you? Bud and Skipper and Early and Mousey."

The boys bowed, and shook hands in a dignified manner. Clearly they were taking their jobs as hosts very seriously.

"I hope you had a pleasant *trip* here," said Mousey in a solemn tone.

The two girls giggled. The ride in the truck seemed very funny now.

"In old Betsy?" asked Skipper. "That thing does nothing but trip and fall apart."

"Oww!" The other boys made horrible faces at the pun, but the ice was broken.

A man in a bright checkered shirt and dungarees rang a cowbell. Soon a number of couples gathered around him. The girls were all dressed in gay skirts and blouses, and low-heeled shoes. The boys wore sport shirts and dungarees. Most of the people seemed older than Donna and Ricky.

"I'm glad Bunny and Dorothy lent us these skirts," whispered Ricky. "It's bad enough to be the youngest ones here—but suppose we weren't dressed right!" She looked horrified at the thought.

The man who held the cowbell divided the couples into groups of four.

"For you people who ain't never square-danced, I'll run you through some of the steps first," he called.

In a few minutes the girls had learned to promenade, to sashay left and sashay right, to allemande and do-si-do.

With the music, however, things went at such a rate that the girls were in a constant state of fear that they would forget the commands.

At the end of the first dance, they were flushed and breathless.

"Oh, that was fun," gasped Donna. "But I felt that I needed two more feet and four more hands."

"I felt I had four hands too many," said Bud shyly. "Gee, I guess I'll never learn this stuff."

"You did very well," Ricky defended him stoutly. "The mistakes were all my fault."

Bud looked at her gratefully. "You think we could try the next one together, too?" he asked bashfully.

"You've improved a lot," Ricky congratulated him when the intermission was called. "Say, that was really hard work."

"While there's some time, how about walking over to the

office?" asked Richard. "Ralph is probably there working on the camp newspaper. And you girls will have a chance to see a little more of the camp."

Donna, Ricky, Bud, and Richard strolled down the hill in the pleasant starry night. Some distance away from the bunks, all alone on the side of the hill, was another cabin which the girls had not seen before.

A light was burning in the cabin, and as they came closer they could see Ralph's lean figure stooping over a desk.

"He would have come to the dance tonight, but his girl couldn't come. So he said he'd rather stay here and work," explained Richard, as they climbed up the three steps to the office.

Ralph invited them in, and showed them the various things of interest—the trophies the boys had won in other years, the pictures of various camp groups, the collections of rocks and butterflies the boys had made.

"Let's sit on the porch until it's time to go back," Richard suggested, when Ralph had finished. "It's awfully stuffy in here."

"Are you suggesting that I'm just a bag of hot air?" Ralph pretended to be hurt. "Just for that, I'll join you on the porch, even though I haven't been asked."

Richard clapped him on the back. "Old man, you're always welcome. Come and tell us about those horrible things you cut up in med school."

Ralph grinned. Then he turned serious. "Talking about med school, I had a very interesting conversation with Doctor Duval when I was at your camp, Donna."

"I'll bet you talked about Johnny," interrupted Ricky.

"That's right." Ralph looked surprised. "Oh, I forgot you're one of his counsellors. Tell me, has he improved at all?"

The girls related the events of the campfire. Ralph listened intently.

"But really," Ricky finished, "we know very little about Johnny. What kind of sleeping sickness would make him act like that?"

Ralph leaned forward. "It's called encephalitis," he said.

Ricky nodded vigorously. "That's it, Donna. En-sef-a-lie-tis. I'll never remember such a long name." Then she turned to Ralph again. "Why won't he talk, though?"

"That's just the point," Ralph said eagerly. "It's a most amazing case. You see, it's a brain disease. But usually the child becomes what you would call 'bad.' That is, he hits other children, gets into a lot of trouble, and seems generally wild. With Johnny the disease seems to have had just the opposite effect. I wonder if he'll ever really recover."

The cowbell interrupted their conversation.

"We'd better hurry back," Richard said. "We don't want to miss the rest of the dance."

"Where do you boys swim?" asked Donna, as they started to climb the hill to the barn.

"Right over there," Richard replied, pointing to his right. "It's really a creek that's been damned up. The bottom is muddy, and grass grows all around the edges, but the water still feels good on a hot day. How's about going over and taking a look?"

"Won't it be out of our way?" asked Donna.

"You can't see anything at night anyhow," added Bud. "I want to see if I remember that sashay stuff."

"Oh, it'll only take a minute," Richard insisted. "It isn't far."

He seemed so anxious that the others agreed to go along. As they reached flat ground they could see the moon reflected on the water.

"Now be careful to go around when you get to this part," Richard called, "because if you don't—" There was a loud thud and a splash!

"What happened, what happened?" shrieked Ricky.

"Richard, where are you?" called Donna.

Bud ran ahead.

"I'm—blop—all right—blop!" came a voice from the water. Then there was the sound of a body struggling.

"Wait a minute," called Bud. "I'll get you out."

But before the second boy had a chance to move toward him, Richard's dripping figure appeared at the edge of the water.

"That was just plain dumb," he admitted sadly. "I was so busy warning you to look where you were going that I didn't pay any attention myself. Now I've spoiled your whole evening, I guess."

"You've done no such thing," protested Donna. "Can't you just go up to your bunk and change your clothes?"

"Sure," Bud agreed. "I'll help you, and the girls can wait outside for a minute. Then we'll be all set."

"Lucky it's a warm night," mumbled Richard as they trudged toward the cabins. "You girls wait near the flagpole, and I'll be out in a minute."

Sounds from the barn reached the girls as they stood near the cabins. Even at that distance, everything seemed gay and lively.

"I hope they won't be too long," Ricky said, tapping her foot. "It's been a wonderful evening so far."

Even though the boys rushed, and they all practically ran the entire distance to the barn, there were only a few dances left.

"Where were you hiding?" asked the other boys. "We wanted to dance with Donna and Ricky, too."

Richard explained what had happened, and the boys teased him as they all walked to the mess hall.

"You really didn't miss much," Skipper consoled them. "Eating's the best part of a dance, anyhow."

And when the girls entered the big log cabin, they were almost ready to agree with him.

The long trestle tables were spread with bowls of salads and platters of cold meats. Everyone helped himself and then found a seat at one of the benches along the sides of the room.

"I guess it was all that excitement that gave me such an appetite," Donna said, as she accepted Richard's offer to fill her plate a second time.

"Now I can understand why you boys are so hungry all the time," commented Ricky. "It must be the clean, fresh air around here."

"That reminds me," said Donna. "We'd better not forget that we have to be back by midnight."

"It was a marvelous evening," Donna said to Richard, glancing at his watch. "But with old Betsy, you never know what'll happen, so we'd better leave now."

As the girls said their good-bys, Richard went to fetch Ralph, who was still working in the office.

"I certainly hope nothing more happens tonight," Donna confided to Ricky. "I've had all I can take for one evening."

But when the truck reached the main road and suddenly stopped dead, the girls realized that the evening was not yet over for them.

Ralph stepped on the starter several times. The motor sputtered, then stopped.

"I do hope we get back on time," worried Donna.

"It's sort of spooky out here, isn't it?" shivered Ricky.

"At least there aren't any haunted houses around," laughed Richard. "Say, Donna, that reminds me. Have you learned anything about your deserted house?"

Donna pointed to Ralph, then put her finger to her lips. Richard nodded to show that he understood.

"Hey, Richard," called Ralph just then. "Look around

there and see if you can find a tin can marked 'Gasoline.'
I'll bet those stupid guys forgot to put gas in when I told
them, and they know this gauge doesn't work."

To the relief of the girls, the can was found, and Ralph
proved to be correct. After a few minutes the truck started
again and in a short while was pulling into the Cherrydale
road.

"It was a marvelous evening," Donna said to Richard.
"I'll always remember it."

"Thanks a lot, Donna," the boy answered.

"Oh, yes." Ricky was still dreaming. "A square dance,
a near drowning, and a stalled truck, all in one night."

"Come on, goof." Donna gave her a push. "These boys
have to get back."

After more thanks to Richard and Ralph, the girls
turned and tiptoed into the house.

"Anyhow, we made it on time," whispered Donna.
"Thank heavens for that."

Miss Patton was still waiting up for them.

"Nancy hasn't stirred, and neither have your girls," she
replied in answer to Donna's question. "A very quiet evening."

"Well, ours certainly wasn't quiet," whispered Donna.

"I'll tell you about it tomorrow. And I'll never forget what you've done for me."

"Oh, shoo," said Miss Patton, as she left.

"So much happened in one night," Donna thought drowsily. "I can't ever remember having such a good time."

She turned on her side and lay very still.

CHAPTER 14 *Someone on the Stairs*

Donna awoke with a start. The moon was shining in patterns on the floor and everything was still. What had awakened her? Then she heard it again. Someone was moaning, right in the room. She sat up and listened carefully. Quietly she slid out of bed, and tiptoed over to the children.

Beth was tossing in her sleep. She seemed to be having a bad dream, and Donna realized that she was making a low sound.

Gently she touched the child's shoulder.

"Bethie, Bethie," she said softly. "Wake up, honey. Everything's all right."

The little girl opened her eyes slowly and looked around.

"Oh, Aunt Donna," she whispered, "I was having a dreadful dream, all about a bear that was chasing me—"

"It's all over now, honey. Would you like a drink of water?"

Beth nodded. "But leave the light on, Aunt Donna, so I can see."

Since the bedroom light would wake the other children, and the hall light was too far away, Donna decided to leave the bathroom light on.

Beth took a sip of water. "Thanks, Aunt Donna," she murmured drowsily, and in a minute was fast asleep.

"I think it's safe to turn off the light now," Donna reasoned. She tiptoed back to the bathroom, her mind returning to the events of the evening. "I think I was dreaming that I was still square-dancing," she thought sleepily, as she reached up to pull the chain on the light.

Her hand froze in mid-air.

She wasn't quite sure what it was that she had heard, but prickles had gone up and down her spine. She was wide awake now, and listening hard. She waited another minute and heard nothing. Just as she was ready to think she had imagined it, she heard it again—a slow creak on the stairs, as though something heavy had rested on a board.

"On the stairs?" she thought, trying to quiet her fears. "Why, Donna Parker, that's ridiculous. Everyone is sound asleep. It must be two o'clock in the morning."

But deep down in her heart she knew that sound of creaking stairs only too well. She had complained of it so many times when she was trying to get the children to sleep, and the people walking up and down the stairs had disturbed them.

For a few minutes, there was utter silence.

"Sometimes a board creaks for absolutely no reason," she decided. "Now listen here, Donna, there's absolutely no one or nothing on the stairs. Go back to bed."

But just then the sound was heard again, this time definitely closer—another slow creak, then silence.

"I must keep calm," she said to herself, but the pounding of her heart grew so loud that she could hardly bear it.

"If it were someone who belonged here, he certainly wouldn't walk so slowly," she thought. "He'd just walk up normally. So it must be someone who *doesn't* live here."

Wild notions of thieves and bandits crossed her mind.

Suddenly she thought of the deserted house, and the light she had seen.

"If anybody really is staying there, they'd know about Cherrydale. They'd know that the porch door here is never locked. And they could find a way to get past the dogs, I

guess. It would be a simple matter to walk in, and up the stairs."

She remembered the queer old man she and Ricky had met at the bridge. "Maybe that's who it is," she thought in panic, "or maybe it's someone even—worse!"

Her eyes were wild with terror. If she could only call someone!

"Help!" Her lips formed the word, but no sound came from her throat.

Then the creak came again, and this time it was quite near.

"I must do something, I must!" she thought wildly. "But I'm in the light, and whoever is out there is in the dark. So he'd see me before I saw him. No, I can't go out there."

She waited, poised for flight. Her heart was hammering, her throat dry. "The children, the children!" she thought. "I must protect them. Oh, help me, somebody, please help me!"

For a long time there was no sound. But now Donna could sense the presence of someone quite near her. There was complete stillness throughout the house. She could picture the sleeping figures. But here she was, in a brightly lighted bathroom, shivering in terror, and there was no one to come to her aid.

"If only one of the children would call, it might scare—him," she thought. "Or if Doctor Duval would wake up, or the dogs would bark." But nothing happened.

Could she really hear breathing near the top of the stairs, or was she imagining it?

"But I'm not imagining the creaking," she told herself. "I'm positive I heard that."

She looked around. Was there something she could use to defend herself? Toothbrushes, soap, towels? She had a wild desire to laugh.

"Can't you picture me pointing a toothbrush at that—person—and yelling 'Stick 'em up'? I can just see the head-lines: Girl Counsellor Uses New Weapon to Defend Camp from Burglar."

Her mind raced on, but one part of it kept listening for the sound. Then it came again, and Donna could tell that it was from the top of the stairs.

She froze again. "Who—who—" She tried to get the words out, but none came.

She glanced at herself in the mirror. Her face was dead white, except for two spots of color high on her cheeks,

Her breath was coming quickly and unevenly.

"I can't stand this any more, I just can't," she thought weakly. "I feel as though I'm going to faint."

With one last desperate effort, she gathered all her strength. She tried to shout, but her voice instead was a faint croak.

"Who's—who's there?" she called.

CHAPTER 15 *Bunny's Problem Solved*

The footsteps came toward the bathroom. Donna held tight to the edge of the sink, and tried to keep from screaming. She closed her eyes.

"Why, Donna!" said a woman's mild voice.

Donna opened her eyes. "It's—it's Mrs. Bond!" she said in amazement. Her knees went weak with relief.

Mrs. Bond stood in the doorway, and clutched her bathrobe to her. "I didn't hear you get back, Donna," she whispered nervously. "I thought Miss Patton was still with your little girls."

"I guess I'd forgotten that you were still here," Donna answered, realizing how unnecessary her fright had been. With all the annoyance that Nancy's mother had caused, and her constant arguments with everyone, how could Donna have forgotten that she was still here, sleeping in

209

the little guest room downstairs!

But why all this secrecy? Why had Mrs. Bond come up the stairs in so mysterious a fashion? She had to find out.

As though reading her thoughts, Mrs. Bond started to explain. "I thought I'd better tiptoe up to the third floor, and see for myself how Nancy was getting along."

Donna knew that Miss Patton was the one person who stood no nonsense from Mrs. Bond. She could understand why Mrs. Bond did not want the nurse to hear her go up the stairs in the middle of the night.

"What made you think that there was something wrong?" Donna asked.

The woman leaned forward. "I heard someone moaning upstairs, and people walking around. Of course my first thought was of Nancy."

Donna tried to keep from giggling. She had really brought all this on herself.

"It was Beth who was moaning, Mrs. Bond, and the people you heard was just me, getting her a glass of water."

Mrs. Bond heaved a sigh of relief. "Oh, I'm so glad that's all it was. You can understand how I felt, though. Imagine leaving my sick Nancy all alone on the third floor!"

"Yikes!" thought Donna. "From the way she talks, you

might think her darling daughter was on a desert island in the middle of the Pacific Ocean." But all she said was, "Why, Miss Patton could have heard her if she called. Besides, she's been upstairs for hours."

"Miss Patton might have been sound asleep," the woman retorted, drawing herself up. "No one but a mother could understand my feelings. Anyhow, I just decided to tiptoe past the nurse, and see for myself."

"And almost scared me to death doing it," thought Donna. She reached for the light chain.

Mrs. Bond turned to go. "I certainly will be glad to get my poor child away from here. We're leaving tomorrow, you know."

"Really?" said Donna politely. "I'm sure you'll be much happier with Nancy at home."

"Indeed I will!" declared Mrs. Bond. "Never again will I let her be so far away from me. A child needs a mother's care and protection."

Donna went back to bed. "I almost feel sorry for Nancy," she thought as she pulled the covers over her. "Imagine having a mother like that!"

She listened for a minute, but all was quiet at last. The four little girls were breathing softly. There was only the sound of the crickets chirping, and an occasional frog croaking.

The events of the night, though, had thoroughly awakened Donna. She lay there thinking. "It seems impossible that just a few hours ago, Ricky and I were getting ready to go to the square dance. It was such a nice evening, too. Wait'll I tell Ricky what happened tonight! Here I was, scared to death practically, and it turned out to be that silly Mrs. Bond tiptoeing up the stairs. I'll bet no mystery writer would ever think of a solution like that." Her thoughts wandered back again to the footsteps on the stairs.

At last she felt herself beginning to get drowsy. "That's one mystery solved," she thought as she turned over on her side. "Now if the mystery of the house in the woods could only be solved as easily— I simply must find out what's going on."

But by morning, with very little sleep behind her, and Bunny not yet returned from her day off, mysterious houses somehow did not seem terribly important.

"Will Aunt Bunny be back soon?" asked Beth, as she struggled to tie her shoes. "I thought she was only supposed to be gone for one day."

"That's right, dear," replied Donna, coming to the

child's rescue and tying the bow. "She'll be here right after breakfast." She was glad that Beth said nothing about the night before, and seemed to have forgotten her bad dream.

Sure enough, just as the children were finishing their milk, Bunny appeared in the doorway. She waved to Donna and the little girls.

"Why, she looks positively beautiful," thought Donna. "Her cheeks are rosy, and her eyes are sparkling. She looks almost like a different person!"

Donna tried not to rush the children away from the table, but she was eager to talk to Bunny.

"What could have happened, to change her so in such a short time?" she wondered.

But Bunny refused to say much. "I'll tell you later," she confided. "It's a long story, Donna, and I can't talk in front of the children. But it has a happy ending."

"I can tell that just from looking at you," smiled the younger girl. "Maybe we'll get a chance to talk during rest hour. And whatever it is, I'm so glad for you, Bunny."

After dinner, as they were taking the children upstairs to rest, Bunny said, "Wait for me on the porch when you're through, Donna, and I'll tell you the whole story."

But as Donna came down the stairs, Mrs. Duval met her.

"Donna, I'd like you to come into the office for a minute," she said.

Donna followed her, puzzled as to the reason. "Now what did I do wrong?" she wondered. Mrs. Duval's tone had not sounded very friendly.

In the office, Mrs. Bond and Nancy were standing by their suitcases. Mrs. Duval left them, and closed the door as she went out.

"Why did Mrs. Duval leave?" asked Donna in surprise.

Mrs. Bond came close to Donna, and placed a hand on her arm. "I told her I wanted to speak to you *privately*," she said, stressing the last word. "I kept thinking of the way you looked last night when I saw you upstairs." She still had an air of secrecy about her. "My dear child, you didn't look at all well."

"I'll admit I was a little upset," smiled Donna. Didn't Nancy's mother have any idea of how scared she had been?

"I decided to do something for you," the woman said. "How would you like me to take you home, away from all this?" She looked around her distastefully.

"You mean right now?" Donna could hardly believe her ears.

Mrs. Bond nodded. "After all, you are a neighbor. I

know how unhappy you must be here, too."

"Oh, no," Donna protested. "I'm not at all unhappy! In fact I'm having a very nice summer." As she said it, she realized how true it was. Why, she would hate to leave Cherrydale. She loved the children, she had made new friends, and she was having a wonderful time.

Mrs. Bond looked at her. "I thought I'd give you this chance, Donna. I don't understand how your parents let you stay at this dreadful place. If you were my daughter, I'd insist that you come home. I can't, however, do that—" her voice trailed off uncertainly.

"I really meant what I said, Mrs. Bond," said Donna firmly. "Thank you very much for your offer. I know you thought you were doing me a favor. But I simply wouldn't consider leaving, and I'm sure my mother would agree with me. It would be nice if you would call my family, though, and tell them that I am well and happy."

Mrs. Bond raised her eyebrows. "That's what happens when people try to help," she said angrily. "I only did this for your own best interests. It really means nothing to me whether you go or stay." She shrugged her shoulders, picked up her suitcase, and opened the door.

Nancy followed her mother. At the doorway the child

turned to Donna. "My mother is going to take me to a fancy hotel at the seashore, where I don't have to make my own bed every day. And I can have ice cream even for breakfast, if I want it. Not like this stinky old camp. Yaah!" She made a face at Donna and left.

Donna stood motionless, wondering what to do next. Mrs. Duval came out of the guest room, where she had been waiting. She put her arm around the girl.

"Donna, dear," she consoled her, "don't worry about the Bonds. There are some people who make nuisances of themselves wherever they go. Either they can't be changed, or they don't want to change. We're really very lucky that they decided to leave. And I'm so glad that you're staying."

Donna looked at her in surprise. "You knew what she wanted to say to me? And you let her talk to me anyhow?"

Mrs. Duval smiled at the girl. "I had a pretty good idea why she wanted to see you. And I felt it was a decision you had to make for yourself. I realize that you're a little young to spend a whole summer away from home, working with small children. But you're doing an excellent job. And I'm proud that you decided to stay."

Donna felt closer to Mrs. Duval than she ever had before. "She doesn't say much," she thought, "but she must notice everything. And she really can be awfully nice. Wait'll I tell Ricky that she actually praised me! The Duvals couldn't possibly be the villains that we thought they were."

Suddenly she remembered Bunny, waiting on the porch.

"I thought you'd never come," said Bunny, who was sitting on the glider with her knees tucked under her. "What was all the excitement about?"

"Just those silly old Bonds. I'm sure Cherrydale will be a lot more peaceful now that they've left."

"Mrs. Bond was practically purple when she got in her car, she was so mad," continued Bunny. "Why were you in the office with her?"

"Oh, Bunny, it was just a bunch of nonsense. What I'm really interested in is you. Please tell me all about everything."

Bunny patted the cushion next to her. "Come and sit down here, and I'll tell you the whole long story."

Bunny took a deep breath. "You must have thought I was pretty crazy this summer," she began. "I suppose I walked around here with a face a mile long."

Donna nodded but remained silent.

"You know," continued the girl, "that I go to college.

I guess I must seem pretty grown-up to you, but I'm only nineteen. And believe it or not, I'm still a baby to my parents."

"My goodness," thought Donna. "I guess you have to be a grandmother for your mother and father to think you're grown-up."

"Anyhow," Bunny went on, "they thought I was much too young to think of being married."

"Married!" Donna sat bolt upright on the swing. "Bunny, I had no idea! *Are* you married?"

"Of course not. But honestly, we were thinking about it, Frank and I. He's graduating from college next June. And oh, Donna, he's so wonderful! Tall, and handsome, and so very nice!" She had a dreamy look in her eyes.

"What's wrong about getting married to someone like that?" asked Donna. "He sounds perfect."

Bunny turned to Donna. "Maybe you're too young for me to tell all these things. But I did want you to understand. You see, my parents thought it was something I'd get over. They made me promise not to see him at all this summer, but to come here again. They thought I'd forget him, because I had such a good time here last year."

"You did?" Donna was amazed. "But this year all you

did was lie around your room and mope."

"That's just it," explained Bunny. "Believe it or not, I could have had a lot of dates even out here. And when my folks explained things to the Duvals, they said I could have as many late nights as I wanted—within reason, of course. But I just didn't want any."

"You mean you could have gone to dances and things, and you preferred to stay here?" It was hard for Donna to understand.

"Exactly," said Bunny. "If I couldn't go out with Frank, I didn't want to see anyone. I even promised not to write to him, and that was hard to do. I was just miserable."

"Then why are you so happy now?" asked Donna. "How did your day at home change you?"

"I felt that things would have to be settled on my day off. I just couldn't stand it any longer, and I knew Frank would be in Summerfield that day. When Mother and Dad saw how miserable I was, we all had a long talk—Frank's family and mine. And guess what!"

"I give up!"

"We're announcing our engagement at the end of the summer, and we'll be married as soon as Frank graduates next June!"

Donna threw her arms around the older girl's neck. "Oh, Bunny, I'm so thrilled! It's simply marvelous. Aren't you *excited?*"

Bunny hugged her warmly. "Now, what do you think? I can hardly wait till camp is over. Poor Frank—he has a summer job about a hundred miles from here, and he won't be able to get back again until the end of August. But he'll be here for the big program."

"Can I see him then?" asked Donna wistfully.

"You'll be the first one to meet him, honey," promised Bunny. "After all, you're the one who had to stand for my nonsense all summer, so you deserve something."

"And that clears up another mystery," decided Donna later. "I have a feeling that pretty soon everything will be solved."

She had no way of knowing that the mystery of the house would deepen, before it was finally settled.

CHAPTER 16   *The House Again*

"I almost hate to leave tomorrow," said Ricky the next night, as the girls were getting ready for bed.

"But it's your day off!" exclaimed Donna, as she hung four pairs of wet little socks on a bar in the bathroom. "Just think, no socks to wash, no mouths to feed."

"I'll bet I miss a lot, too," replied Ricky. "It'll be just my luck not to be here when something exciting happens."

"You can't really mean you don't want to go home, Ricky. And I can almost promise you that things will be very dull. I'll save all the excitement for you when you return." She smiled. There were times when it was hard to resist teasing Ricky.

A little while after the lights had been turned off, Ricky was surprised to find Donna standing over her bed. The redheaded girl almost leaped out of bed.

"What is it, what's happened?" she asked.

Donna motioned for her to lower her voice. "You'll wake everyone," she whispered. "And Bunny and Dorothy are asleep already. Come with me and I'll show you."

Ricky tiptoed after her, back to the pink room. "You don't even have to tell me," she said as Donna pointed to the window. "It's the light again."

"Look for yourself," Donna whispered.

Ricky looked out, past the playground, at the wooded area in the distance. The light could be seen clearly.

"I just knew it," she wailed. "Something was bound to happen. And we were right; it seems to be exactly where the deserted house is."

"We'll go together some day, and see if we can find out what it is," suggested Donna.

Ricky looked at her in astonishment. "You can't do that, Donna. Don't you see? Someone is in that house right now. If we wait too long, whoever it is might have left. We don't even know whether it's one person or a lot of people who use that light."

"I can't go alone, Ricky. You'll have to come with me."

"Oh, Donna, we simply can't sit around and let this mystery slip right through our fingers. I'd die of curiosity, besides. I'll be gone tomorrow, and I'm on duty for the next two afternoons. And by that time it might be too late. No, you've just got to go tomorrow afternoon."

Donna nodded solemnly. She almost wished they had never gone for a walk and had never seen the old deserted house. She wished she had never noticed the light through the trees.

"I'll probably get myself in a peck of trouble," she thought, as she tossed and turned, when Ricky had gone back to bed. "It's in the woods, where we're not supposed to go. Goodness only knows what's in that house. And what'll I do if I find out that there's a dangerous gang hiding out?" She began to tremble. "I'll end up being kidnaped or something. No, I simply won't go. I'll tell Ricky in the morning."

She lay quite still. Then she sat up in bed and stared thoughtfully at her toes. "Let's face it," she sighed after a while. "I'm just as curious as Ricky. Tomorrow might be my last chance to find out about the house. And I'd probably never sleep another wink if I didn't go."

Her mind at rest, she immediately fell asleep.

Ricky did not let her forget her promise. As she left the next morning, she whispered, "Be sure you take something to defend yourself, Don. I'll be thinking about you every minute."

Donna shivered. Ricky was a fine friend, leaving all the dangerous work for her.

"Now, that isn't fair," she said to herself. "Ricky probably envies you. She'd love to be going, too."

At the noon meal, Bunny looked at her strangely. "Whatever has gotten into you, Donna?" she asked. "You're as nervous as a cat!"

"Am—am I?" Donna answered, trying to smile. "Oh, it's nothing. Just a little stomach-ache."

That part was quite true. Her stomach was bouncing up and down like a rubber ball.

As the time drew near for her to leave, however, she found herself growing calmer. It was as though someone were behind her, pushing her along.

She strolled carelessly over to the playground. No one was about. Glancing quickly around, she made a quick dash for the woods, and in a second was hidden by the thick growth of trees and underbrush.

"Now to find the house," she thought. "It would be dreadful if I spent the whole afternoon wandering around in the woods."

She turned around, to see if she could tell in what direction the camp was.

"If I can figure out which is my bedroom window, I'll just keep going toward the place where the light seemed to be," she thought. "That ought to take me to the old house."

But it was useless to try to find the farmhouse. She was completely surrounded by tall trees which kept out any view of the clearing near the playground.

"Oh, dear," she thought. "That idea certainly was no good. I'll just have to trust to luck."

A few steps later, however, she found what seemed to be a narrow path. "If I were an Indian, I'd probably be able to tell a lot by looking at the footprints and the broken branches. But I can't even tell whether the path was made by animals or people."

If she tilted her head far back, she could see bits of blue sky at the top of the trees. "Somewhere out there," she thought wistfully, "people are eating and talking and swimming and walking. Nobody but Ricky knows that I'm here alone in these deep dark woods."

She had come almost to the end of the path. Ahead of her she caught a glimpse of something through the arching

branches. It was the deserted house!

Thank goodness she had found it without too much trouble. On second thought, she did not know whether to be happy or sad. Her heart beat faster. Now came the true test of her courage.

She stepped out from the protection of the trees. Everything was still. Growing bolder, she walked over to the front of the house. She remembered that the front windows had been boarded when they had seen the house the first time. The boards had not been touched.

Boldly she walked up the three steps to the front door. The iron knocker was rusty from years of disuse. She could tell for stretching from the handle to the door jam was a large spider web.

"The door couldn't have been used recently," Donna decided, "or the spider web would have been torn." She felt very proud of her deduction.

Now she was even more confused. If no one were using the queer old house, where did the mysterious light come from?

"I'd better not come to any conclusion until I make a complete investigation," she thought. "But I'm sure no one has been using the front entrance."

As she walked around the house she noticed that the other windows were not covered. "If the side I'm on now faces the farmhouse, I could see a light coming through one of these windows." She tried to peer inside, but layers of dust and dirt prevented her from seeing anything.

"Oh, pooh! It's probably all a case of imagination. I'm quite sure there's no one around. Who would ever think of living in a house where you can't even see out of the windows?"

She walked to the back of the house. Suddenly she stiffened. Something was different back here. A sound, a smell—what was it that had made her stop?

Then she saw it—a pile of tin cans a short distance from her feet. And from them came a thin wisp of smoke, as though someone had recently tried to burn them!

Her first thought was to run back to the shelter of the woods.

"That would really be foolish," she decided, "after I've gotten this far. I may solve the whole mystery in the next few minutes."

Carefully she stepped through the woods to the back door. She lifted her hand to the latch, and then paused and listened.

There was a muffled sound of footsteps coming from inside the house.

Throwing caution to the winds, she dashed around the corner of the house, and flattened herself against the wall. The sound of a creaking door was heard, then a man's heavy footsteps.

The footsteps seemed to go in the opposite direction. Donna waited a moment. Then, curiosity getting the better of her, she poked her head around to see who had come out of the house.

To her amazement, there was nothing—and no one—to be seen. Whoever had come out had disappeared. Was it safe to explore the house now? Or were there more people still inside?

In the distance, something caught the corner of her eye. She moved forward a step, and saw a shadow among the trees. Hardly daring to breathe, she waited. On the other side of the house, where the woods continued, someone was moving in and out among the trees. It must be the person who had come out of the house.

"I've gone this far, so I guess I might as well go a little further," Donna thought. Being sure to keep a careful distance between them, she took the path along which the figure was walking and started to follow him.

Once, when he turned around, she was certain he had caught a glimpse of her. She ducked quickly behind a large tree and stood motionless. But in the split second that she had seen his face, she had recognized him.

"It's the man we met at the bridge! Then he does have something to do with the mystery after all!"

She remembered his curious behavior that day, and again was tempted to return to the camp immediately. "I guess Ricky would never forgive me," she thought. "And I'd never forgive myself," she added.

She could tell that the man was coming to a clearing. Slipping from one tree to another, she came as close to him as she dared.

They were at the bridge. Indeed, the man was standing, his head bowed, exactly as she had seen him the first time.

"If all he's going to do is stand there and look at the water, I won't learn anything here," Donna decided in a few minutes. "Maybe I can go back and take another look at the house."

She turned to leave. At that instant, the man looked up. Even at that distance, she could see the startled expression in his eyes.

"So it is you again," he called. "Come here at once."

Something in his tone made Donna obey.

Slowly, her knees shaking, she went toward the man at the bridge.

CHAPTER 17 *The Man on the Bridge*

The man leaned back against the railing of the little wooden bridge and waited for Donna to reach him. Even when she stood directly in front of him, he did not say a word, but looked her up and down.

Finally he heaved a weary sigh. He put a finger under her chin and looked at her frightened eyes.

"What is your name?" he asked.

"D-Donna Parker," she stammered.

"What do you want with me?" he asked. "Why do you follow me? You think I do not see you through the trees?"

Donna lowered her head. "I-I'm sorry," she said at last. "I didn't mean to bother you."

"Oh, dear," she thought. "This isn't turning out at all as I planned. I'm supposed to be asking him the questions. But now that I'm here, I can't think of anything to say."

"Bother—always there is someone to bother me. Always there is someone looking—looking. Can I not find the peace even here in the quiet woods?"

His shoulders sagged and his shaggy white mustache trembled.

"Goodness!" thought Donna wildly. "I do believe he's almost crying. I certainly would never have believed a thing like this could happen." Aloud she said, "I'm awfully sorry I disturbed you. I didn't know you wanted to be alone. My friend and I just wanted to find out what was going on in the deserted house."

"Ah-ha! So you were solving a mystery, yes? And I was in the middle of the mystery, yes? But what am I doing there, you want to know?" He had spoken softly at first. Now his voice was scarcely a whisper. He sighed again and seemed lost in thought.

Then his voice changed. "Come, sit down here with me, my young lady. First I must find out about you, before I tell you about me. You live near here, no?"

"I'm spending the summer at Cherrydale, taking care of four little girls."

"Ah, yes," replied the man. "The first time we met, you told me all about the Cherrydale. And do you like living at the Cherrydale, Miss Donna?"

Donna's eyes brightened. "Oh, yes, I do," she answered. "It's the first time I've ever been away from home this long, you see. At first I missed my parents and my home a great deal. But then I got to know the people here, and I made friends with them. Now I'm having a wonderful time. Of course, I still miss Mother and Daddy, but at least I know that I can have a good time with other people, too."

The man was quiet. He looked at her gravely. Then he patted her hand. "You have learned a hard lesson, *ma petite*. One's family comes first. But it is good to have the friends, too." He shook his head sadly and dabbed at his eyes.

More than ever, and without knowing why, Donna felt sorry for this strange but gentle figure.

"And the children?" he asked. "You like being the mother to four little girls?"

Donna smiled. Yes, she did feel like a mother to the children.

She described the four children to him, until it almost seemed that they were there on the bridge, too. As she talked, he asked questions.

"And this Carol, she still is so slow eating her food?" he

asked in a grave tone. He really seemed interested.

"Well, I must say she's improved a great deal since the beginning of the summer," Donna admitted. "But she's still the last one finished at every meal."

"And the little Beth—how you say—she is still skinny?"

"Oh, no!" Donna's eyes danced. "You should see how much better she looks now. Why, she actually has roses in her cheeks!"

The man turned to her and smiled.

"Roses—that is what they remind me of. Some day perhaps I should like to see these four little girls—your four rosebuds."

His tone changed again. Now it was more matter-of-fact, more businesslike. "And how long do you stay at this Cherrydale? You will have to be going to the high school soon again, no?"

"In a very short while," agreed Donna. "And, oh, dear, I'd almost forgotten about the entertainment at the end of the summer."

"What is this that you speak of?" he asked in a puzzled tone.

Donna told him about the program to be held at the end of the season. She even explained about the party to be given

in honor of the group which gave the best entertainment at the end of the season.

"And Doctor Duval said that the counsellors of that group would get a special prize." She told him about her mother's broken sewing machine, and how badly she wanted the prize in order to surprise her family with a new machine.

"But sewing machines, they are expensive, no?" asked the man. "Will the doctor give you so much money to get a new machine?"

Donna was troubled. "I guess not," she said sadly. "But anyhow—" and she brightened again—"at least it'll help. That is, if I win. I'd better hurry and think of something or I won't even have a chance at the prize!"

Suddenly she looked at her watch. "Oh, my goodness," she cried, springing to her feet. "I'd better dash if I want to get back to camp on time. It's almost the end of the rest period."

She held out her hand to the man. "I'm sorry I disturbed you, Mr.—Mr.—"

"Call me Paul," the man answered. He shook her hand. "And do not worry. It was very good for me to talk with you, Miss Donna. Perhaps we will meet again, and I will tell you about the mystery the next time. Now you had better hurry back to Cherrydale."

Donna waved and ran off through the woods past the old house. And as before, her mind raced along with her feet.

"Ricky will be awfully disappointed when she comes back," she thought. "Paul learned a lot about me, but I didn't learn much about him except that he couldn't be a thief or anything like that, and he seems awfully unhappy about something. He didn't give me a chance even to find out why he's living in that old house. I wonder whether the Duvals know that he's there. The whole thing just gets queerer and queerer—"

By now she had reached the playground.

"I'll just barely make it in time," she thought, as she sprinted across the lawn, into the farmhouse, and up to the pink room. The end of rest period was announced as she stood panting in the doorway.

"What happened to you?" asked Bunny. "Suppose Mrs. Duval had asked where you were? It's not like you to go off without saying anything to anybody, Donna. Is something wrong?"

Donna shook her head. "No, everything's fine, Bunny.

I'm sorry if you were worried. I won't do it again."

She hurriedly began to dress the children. They had just awakened and were yawning and stretching.

Something the man on the bridge had said to her leaped into her mind. What was it he had called the children? Rosebuds—that was it! And here, still warm and flushed from their naps, they did look like four little rosebuds, awakening from their long winter's sleep.

Donna jumped as though someone had hit her.

"What happened to you?" asked Bunny, looking up, startled.

"I've got it, I've got it!" cried Donna. "Would it be all right for me to take the children down to the rose garden when they've finished their milk, Bunny?"

Bunny was amazed. "You mean the formal garden by the tennis courts? But we pass there every day, on our way to swimming. Why ever do you want to make a special trip there?"

"I've never really looked at the roses," replied Donna. "And there's something special I want to show the children."

Bunny nodded assent.

Suddenly Donna shook her head. "No, that's not the

way to do it. I'd better go alone first and take the children tomorrow. This has got to be just right." Then she laughed. "I must be acting pretty silly but I guess you don't know what hit me, Bunny. Well, I've finally got an idea for the entertainment!"

CHAPTER 18   *A Rosebud Opens*

The rest of the day passed all too slowly for Donna. Several times Bunny had to call her out of a daze. That evening she decided it was time to take things in hand.

"Hey, Donna. I'm the one who's supposed to be doing the daydreaming, not you. Or are you thinking of announcing your engagement, too?"

Donna shook herself. "No, just thinking. Mother said I had to have a clear idea of what I wanted to do before I begin to plan with the children." Then she looked at Bunny guiltily. "Oh, I didn't mean to keep you out of it, Bunny. It's just that you told me to do it myself. Maybe you feel differently now, though—"

Bunny smiled. "That was our agreement. You do the work, and you get the prize. Of course, I'd love to help, if you want me to."

At that moment a car was heard on the road.

"That must be Ricky," said Donna, running out.

The redheaded girl flung open the door of the automobile, and rushed to her friend.

"Oh, Donna, I worried so much about you that I could hardly enjoy my day at home. I never should have let you go into the woods alone. Are you all right?"

"Of course," the dark-haired girl answered. "But I didn't learn very much, except that the man we met on the bridge has something to do with the mystery."

She waited while Ricky said her good-bys and was settled on the porch. Then she recounted all her adventures of the afternoon.

"And he actually gave me an idea for the program, too," she ended. "Oh, I'm so excited about getting started!"

Ricky threw up her hands. "How do you like that! Here we are, on the verge of solving a terrific mystery about a deserted house in the woods, and all this girl can think about is the entertainment."

"Ssh!" cautioned Donna. "Here come the Duvals."

That ended the conversation, and Donna went to bed thinking of gardens, and flowers swaying in the breeze.

She woke up knowing that something exciting was about

to happen. "I'll just keep my fingers crossed, and hope everything works out all right."

The rose garden that afternoon was at the height of its midsummer beauty. Donna wished she knew the names of the different flowers—white and yellow and pale pink and deep wine red.

The children ran from one bush to another, burying their noses in the lovely blooms.

"Look at this bush," called little Dianne. "It's almost as though it's dancing in the breeze."

Donna held her breath. Now was the time to start.

"Can you dance like the roses?" she asked. Dianne smiled shyly, and nodded and stretched her arms out gracefully above her head.

The other children soon joined her. Following Dianne's example, all four little girls stretched on tiptoes, bobbing and swaying.

"That was fun," said Susan when they stopped. "But I get tired. Do you think the roses get tired, too?"

"When do the flowers sleep?" asked Donna.

"All winter," chorused the children.

"And when the warm sun shines down on them in the spring, what do they do?"

"First they're all curled up tight, and then they get bigger and bigger," suggested Carol.

"I can show you," said Dianne, curling her body into a ball on the ground.

"Bless her!" thought Donna. "I've hardly said a word, and it's working out perfectly."

Dianne slowly, gracefully, uncurled the ball, reaching up toward the sun until she was stretched on her very tiptoes. Her arms flung wide, she turned her pink-and-white face to the sun, as though waiting for it to kiss her.

The children applauded.

"May we do it, too? We want to be rosebuds, too," they clamored.

Donna nodded. This time there were four rosebuds, opening to the warm rays of the sun.

"I can just see them, in pink crepe paper costumes with frilly edges," thought Donna. She tucked the words "pink crepe paper" away in her mind.

The children sank exhausted to the ground.

"It was fun being a rose," said Beth. "But I wouldn't want to be a flower when it's cold."

"Would you like to hear a story about a flower who lived under the ground?" asked Donna. "When I was as old as you, my mother used to tell it to me."

The children seated themselves in a semicircle around her. They listened spellbound while Donna told them of the little rosebud who lived way under the ground, and who was awakened by the sun and the rain tapping on her door.

"I think we could act out that story," said Susan. "Someone could be the rosebud, and someone else the sun, and the rain, and the other rose in the garden. We have just enough people."

Of course everyone wanted to be the rosebud. They finally agreed to let Susan have first chance, since it had been her idea.

"Somehow or other, I'll try to get them to give that part to Dianne," thought Donna. "But really, everything's going along simply beautifully."

When they had finished, Donna applauded.

"That was excellent," she said. "And the rose dance was lovely, too. I'm sorry we didn't have a bigger audience to see you."

"Maybe some day we can do it for the whole camp," suggested Carol.

"Could we have real costumes, like I have for dancing

school?" asked Dianne, jumping up and down excitedly.

Donna nodded. "Of course they couldn't cost a lot of money, and we'd have to make them ourselves."

"Maybe we could make them out of crepe paper. That's what we did at nursery school," said Susan.

Donna could have kissed her. "Oh, that would be just fine, Susan," she said, as though she had never thought of the idea. "How about pink crepe paper, so you'll look like real roses? And in the play, the rain could wear gray—"

"And the sun could wear yellow," interrupted Beth, her eyes shining.

"Oh, won't we look pretty!" said Dianne. "I wish my mother could see us."

"Well, your mothers and fathers are coming to the entertainment on the last day—" began Donna.

"Goody, goody!" cried the children. "Let's do it then, Aunt Donna. We'll practice hard, so it'll be just right. Oh, please say Yes, Aunt Donna!"

Donna nodded. It was almost too perfect. And they really thought that it was all their own idea. Well, in a way she guessed it was.

Miss Patton agreed to buy the colored crepe paper the next time she went into Byersville. The children practiced at every opportunity, and tiptoed around, arms outstretched and swaying.

Bunny watched one rehearsal, and gave her approval. "I'm sure everyone will love it," she said. "They look darling. We'll have to plan some cute costumes, too."

Although Donna hated rainy days because the children had to be kept indoors, she was delighted to see the overcast skies one morning.

"This will be a wonderful chance to start on the costumes," she suggested to Bunny.

"Right after breakfast," Bunny agreed, "we can go right into the recreation room. We can use the Ping-pong table to cut on."

The children were excited, and even Carol gulped her breakfast.

As they were leaving the dining room, Donna caught a glimpse of Ricky.

"What in the world is the matter with you?" Donna asked. "You look as though you've lost your last friend."

"We're rushing like mad to get ready for the entertainment, too," wailed Ricky. "We're having a toy band, you know. Dorothy is showing the boys how to make their own instruments. They're tying bells on sticks, and even making drums. I had no idea so much was involved."

"I'll bet it's an awful lot of work," said Donna. "Are the boys really doing it?"

"All except Johnny—he's my problem. I guess it's too noisy for him—not that I don't agree with him. Anyhow, he just sits in the corner and weeps, won't do a thing. I feel just dreadful about it, and I don't know what to do."

"Wait a second," said Donna. She consulted hurriedly with Bunny, then whispered in Ricky's ear. Ricky looked doubtful. "Well, you could try," she said.

Donna went over to Johnny, and bent down toward him. "Johnny, would you like to help us in the game room? We're going to make costumes out of this pretty crepe paper. See?"

He looked from Donna to Ricky. "It's all right, Johnny. You may go if you'd like to."

His face was wreathed in smiles. He slipped his hand into Donna's, and looked longingly at the brightly colored crepe paper.

"Gee, thanks a million," whispered Ricky, as she ran off. "Let me know if he's any bother."

But Johnny was as gay as a little grasshopper while the paper was unrolled. Donna and Bunny measured and fitted, and the little girls stood patiently.

Then Bunny showed them how to frill the edges of the crepe paper, so that it looked almost like real rose petals.

"See, Johnny, there's a piece for you, too." Donna handed him a large pink sheet and showed him how to ruffle it. He rewarded her with a big grin, and set to work eagerly.

"He really likes you," murmured Bunny. "I've never seen him so happy. You know just how to handle him."

Donna beamed. "I guess I've been around at the right time," she said modestly. "First when he was sick, and then when he was lost in the woods at the campfire—oh, help!" She broke off as she noticed the children struggling with the yellow paper for the sun.

"I'll just have to pin it on you, Susan," she said a moment later to the child, who had cheerfully agreed to let Dianne be the rosebud in return for wearing a yellow crown.

"It just won't stay put," she moaned. "If I pin it right in one place, it slides off in another."

Johnny was watching with interest. Suddenly he slid off his chair and went over to stand beside Donna.

"If only someone would hold the paper right over here," she muttered.

Johnny tapped her on the shoulder.

"I will," he said slowly and distinctly.

Donna almost swallowed a pin. "What—what did you say, Johnny?" She was sure that her ears had deceived her.

"I will help you," he said.

Donna dropped paper, pins, and almost knocked Susan down. She grabbed Johnny and hugged him tightly.

"Oh, Johnny—you talked, you talked!"

CHAPTER 19 *The Big Day*

Bunny looked up. Donna was still holding Johnny.

"Did I really hear that?" asked Bunny.

Donna nodded, too overcome to speak. She swallowed hard. Then she took Johnny by the hand and led him gently to Bunny.

"Tell Aunt Bunny what you just said, dear," she whispered softly.

He looked up at her and she felt that in another second the stricken look would reappear.

"Now I've scared him again," she thought in despair. She knelt down, and began to tell him about the pretty colored paper, and the costumes they would make for the children, and how nice it would be if he would help, too.

"You would like to help us, wouldn't you, Johnny?" she questioned gently.

"Yes," he whispered shyly. "Oh, yes!"

Donna turned to Bunny. "You see? He can speak if he wants to."

Bunny was overjoyed. "Donna, run and tell Mrs. Duval right away," she said. When Donna hesitated, the older girl pushed her toward the door.

In a few minutes Donna returned with Mrs. Duval. Johnny would not say more than a word or two, but it was enough for Mrs. Duval to realize that a wonderful thing had happened.

Ricky and Dorothy were told, too, and soon the news spread throughout the camp.

That evening, Dr. Duval spent a long time with Johnny. After the child had gone to bed, the doctor called Donna into his office.

"Donna," he said in his most serious manner, "you have done for Johnny what no amount of medicine or treatment could do. You have given him back his voice."

Tears rose unbidden to Donna's eyes.

"I don't know what I did, but whatever it is I'm awfully glad." She turned to leave.

"Even though I'm not paid at all, and even if I don't win the prize, I still feel that the summer has been worth it," she thought. "Isn't it wonderful how good it makes you feel when you do something for other people?"

The remaining days passed in a flurry of rehearsing and sewing and costume-fitting. The jingle of rhythm sticks and bells mingled with the beat of toy drums. From the cabins on the hill came the cries of Punch and Judy, in preparation for the puppet show the older girls were giving. And the older boys practiced being clowns and acrobats and bareback riders, for the circus they would put on. Even the rabbits, who were supposed to be lions and tigers in the wild animal act, seemed to feel the excitement in the air.

"Oh, me, oh, my," sighed Ricky one evening, sinking into her accustomed place on the porch glider. "Thank heavens there are only a few more days to go. I don't think I'd be able to stand much more of it. *One*-two-three, *one*-two-three. All together now!" She mimicked herself leading the toy band. "And as soon as you think they're doing fairly well, Freddie decides he wants Eddie's drum, or Charles pulls the bells off his stick. Such fun!"

"Well, you'll feel it was all worth it when your group wins the prize," consoled Donna.

Ricky wrinkled her freckled nose. "Oh, Donna, how

can you say such a thing. I watched your girls do their flower dance, and they looked like four little dolls. They're really adorable. I'm sure you'll get the prize."

Donna, however, was not at all sure that she agreed with Ricky. But by now it hardly seemed important. Every time Johnny spoke, she felt she had been given a reward. And, instead of wanting the day of the entertainment to come quickly, she dreaded having the time pass.

"Remember how scared we were at the beginning of the summer, when we came here?" she reminded Ricky. "Now I'm sure I'll cry when it's time to leave."

"I hope they ask us back for next summer," mused Ricky. "Maybe we'll get a chance to find out then about the house in the woods. Because here it is practically the end of this summer, and we haven't solved the mystery. That's the one thing that bothers me."

Donna nodded agreement. "I would have liked to see that old man again. He was so strange, and I never did figure out what was bothering him. We didn't even learn whether he was living in the old house, or whether the Duvals knew about him."

"It's too late now," commented Ricky, not realizing how much could happen in a few days. "Even on my afternoons off, I work like mad on that toy band. Imagine, working so hard and calling it fun! I sure will surprise my family when I tell them about it."

Donna, too, worked every afternoon. At last the costumes were finished, folded, and put away.

The night before the big day, she and Bunny bathed four little girls, washed four little heads, and sank exhausted into the nearest chairs.

"Well, they're off to bed at last," sighed Donna.

"Mm," murmured Bunny. "Now all we have to do is polish their shoes, wash their socks, lay out their clothes for tomorrow, wash our hair, and take our baths. I'm tired before I begin."

Although Donna was sure she would toss and turn all night, thinking about the next day, she slept soundly from sheer exhaustion.

When the rays of the morning sun warmed her face, she awoke with a start.

"Oh, it's a beautiful day," she yawned. A cool breeze fluttered the curtains, and the sky was as blue as her brother Jimmy's favorite marble. The day gave promise of being a perfect one.

Even at breakfast, a feeling of excitement stirred the

camp. From outside came the sound of folding chairs being unloaded from a large truck. Later they would be put on the lawn near the house, where a gradual slope formed a natural theater. The formal gardens would be the back-drop for the stage.

Long trestle tables were set up on the lawn on the other side of the house. From these, refreshments would be served to the parents and campers when the program had ended.

The girls had never seen Dr. and Mrs. Duval move quite so quickly, and seem to be in so many places at once. The phone rang incessantly, and at last Mrs. Duval asked Ricky to remain in the office to take the calls.

Long before it was time to dress the children in their costumes, parents began to arrive. The hum of voices grew steadily stronger, and no place was safe from the eager in-spection of parents' eyes.

"We'd better close the door to the pink room," suggested Bunny. "Otherwise we'll have fifty mothers and fathers wandering in here while the children are getting dressed. We'd never be ready on time."

Just as the last pink ruffle was smoothed into place, there came a knock on the door. Ricky stuck her head in.

"Someone to see you, Bunny."

Bunny, putting lipstick on Susan's already red lips, turned around. "For me?" Then she dropped the lipstick. "Oh, Ricky—" she turned to Donna—"oh, Donna, here, you finish."

Donna had never seen her so flustered before. Then she understood, when she looked at Bunny's rosy face and sparkling eyes.

"Of course, Bunny. Hurry! And don't forget. You promised to introduce me."

Bunny threw her a kiss and raced out.

"Is Aunt Bunny going to see her daddy?" asked Susan.

"You mean her *husband,*" corrected Beth. "The one she's going to get married to, soon."

"Who told you that Aunt Bunny is getting married?" asked Donna, amazed.

"Oh, we heard," said Carol. "We hear a lot of things."

"I'll bet they do," thought Donna wryly. "I'll bet they know a lot of things we think they know nothing about."

She herded the children down the stairs, to wait in the dining room until the program began.

Bunny was standing in a corner of the room, talking to a dark good-looking young man who towered above her.

When she saw Donna, she took the young man by the arm and led him over to the children.

"Donna, I'd like you to meet Frank. You've both heard a lot about each other, and I'm glad you're able to meet at last."

Donna held out her hand. Frank had a charming smile. And best of all, he treated her like a grownup and not like a child. She would have liked to talk to them longer, but with all the people milling about, conversation was impossible.

She was glad to see that the mothers and fathers of all four little girls had arrived. She knew how disappointed the children would have been otherwise, and only wished her own parents could have come.

Then Mrs. Duval brought another woman over to her, and introduced her as Johnny's mother.

The woman leaned over and kissed Donna. When she spoke, her voice was choked with emotion. "Everyone here has been so wonderful to Johnny," she said. "And Mrs. Duval has told me what you did, and how fond Johnny is of you. My dear, words can never express my thanks."

Donna gulped. She looked at Mrs. Duval, expecting to see her beaming with approval.

But what was this? Something about Mrs. Duval seemed strange. The look in her eyes—was it fear, or wonder, or confusion? Certainly it had nothing to do with Johnny.

Before she had time to look again, Mrs. Duval had dashed off. She must have imagined it; Mrs. Duval was probably upset because of the uproar. But when Donna saw Dr. Duval, she noticed the same strange expression. What was the trouble? What was going on? And why were they watching her?

Then Ricky, looking for the Duvals, passed Donna. "I'm still answering the phone in the office," she whispered. "It hasn't stopped ringing. And the craziest things have been happening!"

Before Donna could question her, Ricky had disappeared.

At that moment the dinner bell rang. The older boys, dressed in their clown costumes, pushed through the crowds in the house calling, "Everyone out on the lawn! Time for the show to begin! Take your seats, please!"

The little girls jumped up and down with excitement. "Come on, Aunt Bunny! We're ready, Aunt Donna! Ooh, we can hardly wait!"

The guests began trooping out onto the lawn. The children, following their instructions, left the house by way of the game room. They were to wait just around the corner of the house until their turn to perform.

Donna peeped around the corner, where she could see what was going on in the "theater." Every seat was taken, and there were a number of people standing behind the rows of chairs.

Donna felt a tap on her shoulder. "Are they here yet?" asked Ricky's voice in her ear. The dark-haired girl whirled around.

"Oh, you startled me, Rick. Is who here yet?"

"The boys—you know, Richard and Ralph and the rest of them."

"But I didn't know—" protested Donna.

"While I was in the office they called," explained Ricky. "They all had the afternoon off and wanted to know if they could drive over. The Duvals gave their permission, and they should be here soon."

"Is that what you meant about crazy things happening?"

"That, and something else. There was a very strange phone call, which really set the Duvals back on their heels. I wish I knew who called."

"Is that why they're acting so funny?" asked Donna.

"They kept looking at me so strangely—not exactly mad, just sort of wondering. You don't suppose anything is wrong at home, do you, Ricky?" Donna frowned and looked troubled.

The red-haired girl patted her arm. "Of course not, Donna. I'm sure it had nothing to do with you. It was a strange man's voice on the phone."

"Line 'em up, girls, line 'em up," called Miss Patton, who was working as hard as any of the counsellors.

The children moved back, taking their places in the order in which they were to appear on the program.

Donna could see very little now, since she had to stay with the four girls. But from the hush that fell over the audience, she could guess that Dr. Duval was ready to introduce the program.

He spoke for several minutes, and then the signal came for the rhythm band.

Ricky clutched Donna. "Oh, Don, I'm as scared as the children. Isn't that silly?"

Donna squeezed her friend's hand. "I'm scared, too. But everyone will be so busy watching the kids that they won't even notice us, anyhow."

Ricky smiled weakly, as the little boys gathered sticks,

bells, and drums, and disappeared on to the "stage."

Much as Donna would have liked to watch the band, she decided to stay with the "rosebuds," since they were next on the program.

"I certainly hope no one loses a skirt," she muttered, crossing her fingers. To make sure, she again inspected pins and sashes. The children twirled around proudly, fluffing out ruffles and perking bows.

"Remember," whispered Donna, "before the play starts, Susan is to put on her yellow crown for the sun, and Beth is to put on her gray crown for the rain."

The children nodded soberly.

In a minute, to the sounds of applause and laughter, the little boys came running back.

Ricky wiped her eyes with a handkerchief.

"Why, Ricky, what's the matter?" asked Donna.

"Didn't you hear? They were—were—*laughing* at us!" she sobbed. "And we worked so hard."

Dorothy came over to the two girls, a big smile on her face. "Ricky, honey, they were laughing because they *liked* it! The children looked so very serious. Even Johnny did just beautifully. And did you see what happened at the very end?"

Ricky shook her head silently.

"The twins, Freddy and Eddie, stood up and, both together, they bowed very low, as though all the applause were just for them. Everyone simply howled."

Ricky brightened. "Then they really did like it, Dorothy?"

"It was just wonderful, honey."

Dr. Duval had finished making the second announcement, and signaled for the little girls.

Bunny and Donna held each other's hands tightly for a second. Then the four little girls tiptoed out to face the audience. At sight of them a murmur of delight passed through the crowd.

"They do look beautiful," thought Donna proudly. And from that moment she knew that everything would be all right.

Never had the four little girls danced more gracefully. Never had they spoken their lines more clearly. They remembered every single thing they had been taught, and all Donna's worries vanished.

To the sounds of thunderous applause, the "rosebuds" tiptoed off the stage.

"Will we win the prize?" asked Carol.

"We tried awfully hard to do everything right for you," added Beth.

"I know you did, dears," beamed Donna. "And it really isn't important whether we win or not. You did just beautifully."

But in a corner of her mind, she could see her mother's face when she was given the prize money. "Here, Mother, this is all for you, to buy a new sewing machine," she would say.

Donna sighed. She had just been fooling herself. The prize really was important, after all.

"Oh, well," she thought, "it's all over, and I've done the best I could. There's nothing to do but wait."

Suddenly she remembered what Ricky had said about the boys from Three Pines. "I wonder whether they arrived," she thought.

She walked a few steps around the corner. Everyone was watching the puppet show being given by the older girls, and she could observe the crowd without being seen.

But before she had a chance to notice whether the boys were there, her eye was caught by someone standing between Dr. and Mrs. Duval. He was an elderly man, dressed in an expensive-looking blue summer suit. His face was tanned, and his thick white hair and small white mustache gave him a distinguished appearance.

"Gee, he must be somebody famous," thought Donna. "I wonder if that's the man who called on the phone, that the Duvals were so excited about. But then, that would have nothing to do with me."

Something about the way the man was standing, motionless and with his head slightly bowed, caused Donna to examine his face intently.

"He looks awfully familiar," she thought. "I'm positive I've seen him somewhere before."

She watched him for a moment. Then her heart almost stopped for a second.

"The man on the bridge—Paul—that's who he looks like! But he couldn't be the same person."

Or could he?

CHAPTER 20 [—] *The Mystery Is Solved*

Donna watched the man, hoping he would turn his face toward her.

Out of the corner of her eye, she saw some hands at the rear of the audience waving wildly. It was the boys from Three Pines, trying to get her attention.

She waved back, then put her finger to her lips and motioned to them to be still. She would have liked to continue watching the mysterious white-haired man, but decided it was wiser to go back to the children.

The puppet show was soon over, and the circus began. The audience applauded again and again, as the boys did tricks with bicycles, stilts, and "wild" animals.

Ricky and Donna listened to the enthusiasm of the visitors and shook their heads.

"They're sure to get the prize," confided Donna. "And

they deserve it, too." But in that little corner of her mind, she could see the beloved sewing machine take wings and fly away.

Then the program was over.

"Please remain seated," called Dr. Duval over the hubbub of voices. "There are several announcements to be made."

He waited a moment for quiet. Then he made the same speech to the audience that he had made at the counsellors' meeting many weeks before.

"This sounds sort of familiar," whispered Ricky, as the doctor came to the part about a job well done being its own reward.

"But," he continued, "we also feel that extra work should carry extra compensation. And after what you have seen here this afternoon, I am sure that you will agree that everyone concerned has worked very hard."

There was wild applause from the audience.

"I am sure you will also agree with us, that to choose one group as the winner, would be grossly unfair to the others. Therefore, I should like to announce that the winner is— the entire camp! *All* the children will be the guests of honor at our party, and—"

He was interrupted, as everyone clapped again.

"And as for the counsellors, if they will come into my office after the party, they will each receive an envelope containing fifteen dollars."

Bedlam broke out among the girls, as they kissed, hugged, and congratulated each other.

Dr. Duval called them on stage, and they all took bows, to the delight of the children.

Even in the midst of the gaiety, Donna noticed that the strange man standing next to Mrs. Duval seemed to be looking straight at her.

"But he's smiling," thought Donna, "and he looks so happy. Even if Paul had his hair and mustache cut, and got new clothes, I still can't picture him looking happy."

People were beginning to rise, when Dr. Duval came before them again. This time, at his side stood the distinguished-looking man in whom Donna was so interested.

Everyone settled back in his chair. Donna noticed the puzzled expressions on all the faces, which clearly said, "Who can this man be?"

"My dear friends," began the doctor, and his voice throbbed with feeling, "I have the great honor to present a very dear friend of mine, who would like to say a few words to you. I present the Comte de la Tour-Pointue."

Everyone gasped.

"A real count!" squealed Ricky. "And right here beside us."

"Ssh!" whispered Donna. So the man was a count. She was thrilled, and yet a little disappointed. It would have been wonderful if he had been Paul.

"Please forgive that I do not speak so well the English," began the count.

Donna clutched Ricky. "Oh," she squealed. "It *is* Paul. I could recognize his voice anywhere."

"You mean the man on the bridge?" whispered Ricky. "Are you sure, Donna?"

Donna nodded. She did not want to miss a word of what he was saying.

"I am in this country of yours for not even one year, and I have not talked much the language. But what I have to say comes from the heart."

A deep silence settled on the crowd. Everyone strained forward.

"Many years ago," he went on, "in a small village in France, there live two small children, a boy and a girl. There is near the town a large chateau—a castle—and the children every afternoon walk to the castle. They pick the flowers that grow on the hillside, and play games among the large rocks. One day the man who lives in the castle, he comes out and sees the two children playing merrily. Then he, too, picks the flowers and plays the games with the little boy and girl every afternoon. They have great fun, and become very good friends."

He paused, as though remembering.

"But, alas, a day comes when the family of the boy goes to America, and only the little girl is left. A little while later, she, too, goes to America with her family. But they do not forget the count. Many letters they write, and when they are grown, they again come to see their old friend."

He looked around, then clasped Dr. Duval's arm. "And do you know who this little boy and little girl are? They are our good friends, Doctor and Madame Duval." There was a sharp intake of breath throughout the audience.

"Look at Mrs. Duval," commented Ricky. "She's actually blushing."

"He's not finished yet," murmured Donna.

"Many times," the count continued, "they come to see their old friends in France, and always they visit the man in the chateau."

He sighed deeply. "But one year they cannot come any longer. There is a war, dreadful war. The enemy comes to France and everyone is afraid. Some people continue to work for freedom, for liberty. The enemy finds them, and—!" The white-haired man took a handkerchief from his coat pocket, and wiped his eyes.

"The count is one whom they find. But he is lucky. They do not kill him. They take him to another country and put him in a prison camp. When the war is over, and France is free again, he is an old man, with white hair." He touched his head.

"But the worst part later he finds out. Back he goes to his home, but there is no home left. There is no village left. There is no family left. Everything the enemy has taken, everything they have destroyed."

Donna found herself wiping her eyes with the back of her hand. "Poor man," she thought. "No wonder he was so sad."

"Everywhere he looks for them—for a daughter, a son, a grandchild, anyone. Many times he thinks he has found someone, but—never is it the right one. For years he looks and then he gives up. What remains? Nothing there is to live for. He does not want to see anyone, to go anywhere, to do anything. He sits and weeps.

"But the story has the—what you call it?—the happy ending. The doctor and his wife find the count. They tell him they will bring him to their country. They promise him a quiet place, a house in the woods. They will not let anyone disturb him. Then they will not have to worry about him. And so he does what they tell him.

"But one day, someone has disturbed him. It is a young girl."

Donna felt her face redden, and hoped no one was watching her.

"She does not mean to bother him. He looks at her, and he remembers his grandchildren. One would be just like her. She tells him of her four little girls at camp, and as he listens again he remembers the happy days at the chateau. Once again he wants to hear the laughter of young voices, to see the beautiful world as a child sees it. So at last he comes out of the house in the woods, and here he is. And to give an old man much happiness, he would like you to meet the young girl who does all this for him."

Someone pushed Donna forward. She found herself next to the count, with his arm around her. There were cheers from the audience.

"And since she has done this for him, he wants to do something that will make her happy. And what will make this charming young girl happy? Wait one moment, and you will see."

Dr. Duval motioned to two of the big boys standing at the back of the crowd. They came forward, lugging a large case.

The boys placed the case on a small stand and at a signal from the count, opened it.

Donna could hardly bring herself to look in the case. When she did, she was too overcome to say a word.

Her dreams had been answered! It really was true! There, before her, was a beautiful, wonderful, gorgeous electric sewing machine!

She flung her arms around the count's neck. A second later, she drew back, embarrassed.

"I'm—I'm sorry. I shouldn't have done that."

The count smiled at her.

"But, oh," she breathed, "how can I ever thank you?"

"It is for me to thank you," he answered with a courtly bow, and kissed her hand.

After that, things happened too fast for Donna to recollect them clearly.

Everyone rushed up to shake hands with the count and to congratulate Donna.

The boys, of course, were first on the spot. They were a trifle overwhelmed, and even Richard was impressed.

"So you're a friend of the count's," he said. "I guess plain people like us won't be important to you."

Donna managed to reassure him, and shook his hand warmly. She even found a minute to tell Ralph about Johnny, knowing how interested he would be.

"So he's finally talking," Ralph said. "I must remember to tell the fellows at med school about him. A most remarkable case!"

She dimly remembered the parents of the four "rosebuds" shaking her hand, and thanking her for the excellent care she had given the little girls all summer.

"I'll miss every one of them," she said a little tearfully. "I've certainly grown to love them."

At the party, the count was by her side almost every minute. She could hardly believe that he was the sad, miserable man who had told her his name was Paul.

And the children did not know whether to be more excited by the refreshments, the guests, or the fact that the count played "Farmer In The Dell" with them.

"He's sort of like a king, isn't he?" Donna remembered Susan saying to her.

"Well, a little bit," Donna had answered, smiling at the chubby little face.

But one thing Donna clearly recalled was her conversation with the Duvals.

"I almost spoiled all your plans," Donna apologized to them. "Now I know why you didn't want us to go into the woods. I suppose I should be punished for disobeying you."

Mrs. Duval smiled. "As it turned out, Donna, it was the best thing that could have happened. Of course, we had an idea that you and Ricky were interested in the house in the woods."

Donna suddenly remembered the night of the square dance. "I wonder how much those girls know," Dr. Duval had said. Wasn't it fortunate they hadn't been stopped then?

"But next time I promise to obey," Donna said. "We might not be so lucky again."

Then there was a flurry of good-bys as everyone began to leave.

First came the boys from Three Pines, who promised to see her in Summerfield; then the children, who kissed her and said they wanted her to be their counsellor the next year; then Bunny and Frank, who informed her that she was invited to their engagement party; and finally the count, who said he would be sure to call her very soon.

Finally she and Ricky were left alone, on the porch glider, too numb with the events of the day to say a word. The Parkers were to come for them the next morning.

Mrs. Duval appeared on the porch.

"Donna," she said, "your mother just called. If you can pack quickly, I think they'll come and get you and Ricky in a little while, instead of waiting for the morning."

Both girls leaped to life. Even before the Parker car drove up to the farmhouse, they were standing on the porch with their trunks beside them, and the sewing machine resting proudly in its case.

"Richard said that this would be an exciting summer," Donna recalled. "Of course, he was only kidding. He didn't know how true it would be."

"And to think I almost spent a summer working in a dry goods store," Ricky said. "That seems a million years ago."

"School seems a million miles away, too," countered Donna. "But before we know it we'll be back. Imagine, at last we'll be seniors at Summerfield Junior High School!"

But a great deal was to happen before Donna actually entered the doors of the school.

The Parkers arrived in a short time, and with the good-bys of the Duvals ringing in her ears, Donna raced out to greet her family.

"Oh, Mother! Oh, Daddy! I've never had such an exciting time in my whole life. Wait'll you hear!"

As they rode back to Summerfield, Donna had no way of knowing that she was racing toward a new, even more thrilling, set of adventures.

Famous Classics

Alice in Wonderland

Fifty Famous Fairy Stories

Little Men

Robinson Crusoe

Five Little Peppers and How They Grew

Treasure Island

The Wonderful Wizard of Oz

The Three Musketeers

Robin Hood

Heidi

Little Women

Black Beauty

Huckleberry Finn

Tom Sawyer

Meet wonderful friends—in the books
that are favorites—year after year

\# 5 Date Due

Fiction for Young People

THE RIFLEMAN

THE RESTLESS GUN

WAGON TRAIN

GENE AUTRY
The Ghost Riders

WYATT EARP

GUNSMOKE

ROY ROGERS
The Enchanted Canyon

DALE EVANS
Danger in Crooked Canyon

ROY ROGERS AND DALE EVANS
River of Peril

DRAGNET

BOBBSEY TWINS
Merry Days Indoors and Out
At the Seashore
In the Country

WALTON BOYS
Gold in the Snow
Rapids Ahead

ANNIE OAKLEY
Danger at Diablo
Double Trouble

NOAH CARR, YANKEE FIREBRAND

LEE BAIRD, SON OF DANGER

CIRCUS BOY
Under the Big Top
War on Wheels

HAVE GUN, WILL TRAVEL

MAVERICK

**ASSIGNMENT IN SPACE
WITH RIP FOSTER**

DONNA PARKER
At Cherrydale
Special Agent
On Her Own

**TROY NESBIT'S
MYSTERY ADVENTURES**
The Diamond Cave Mystery
Mystery at Rustlers' Fort

RED RYDER
Adventures at Chimney Rock

RIN TIN TIN
Rinty
Call to Danger
The Ghost Wagon Train

FURY
The Mystery at Trappers' Hole

LASSIE
Mystery at Blackberry Bog
The Secret of the Summer
Forbidden Valley

WALT DISNEY
Spin and Marty
Spin and Marty, Trouble at Triple-R

TRIXIE BELDEN
The Gatehouse Mystery
The Red Trailer Mystery
The Mystery off Glen Road
The Mysterious Visitor
Mystery in Arizona

Adventure! Mystery! Read these exciting
stories written especially for young readers